KING KONG
THE ISLAND OF THE SKULL

KING KONG
THE ISLAND OF THE SKULL

An original novel

by Matthew Costello

Pocket STAR Books
New York   London   Toronto   Sydney

An *Original* Publication of POCKET BOOKS

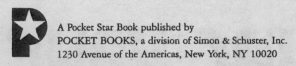

A Pocket Star Book published by
POCKET BOOKS, a division of Simon & Schuster, Inc.
1230 Avenue of the Americas, New York, NY 10020

ISBN-13: 978-1-4165-1669-9
ISBN-10:   1-4165-1669-7

This Pocket Star Books paperback edition November 2005

10 9 8 7 6 5 4 3 2 1

POCKET STAR BOOKS and colophon are registered trademarks of Simon & Schuster, Inc.

Manufactured in the United States of America

For information regarding special discounts for bulk purchases, please contact Simon & Schuster Special Sales at 1-800-456-6798 or business@simonandschuster.com.

To Ray Harryhausen,
who, along with Willis O'Brien,
inspired and amazed and stunned us all . . .

PROLOGUE
A Painted Ship . . .

26 degrees 13 minutes, 45 degrees, 12 minutes

BRADDOCK FELT EVERY RIPPLE in the sea rocking the small boat, bobbing even as the engines tried to make some headway in the choppy water.

His cap barely kept the blazing sun off his face.

Like the others, he had broken out in blotchy patches that cracked, and then turned red and sore, as if they all had stayed out in the sun way too long.

But it's not that, Braddock knew.

The sun had nothing to do with this. No, the first mate on this ramshackle pearl boat knew that something *else* was wrong with the entire crew.

Some of the men hadn't surfaced for breakfast, and the cook barely got through throwing some leftover hash into a pot and declaring it edible.

Something had made everyone on board sick.

And God, he thought . . . *where was the nearest land, the nearest civilized land where we might hope to get some medical attention, something to stop the peeling, the redness, the churning feeling in our guts that made eating an impossibility?*

Braddock licked his cracked lips. There was only one thing to do. The captain had to get them to land.

And fast. But Braddock knew that wouldn't be easy.

He looked up at the amazing blue sky, the golden sun, the brilliant light.

Yeah, if you sat out in the sun for a day it would only burn you; but it couldn't do this, whatever was happening to the crew.

Braddock had an idea what it might be.

He looked at the steering room. Captain up there, all alone.

Braddock wiped his brow, turned, and started for the wheel room.

The captain sat in the tall chair in front of the wheel, staring at the sea. He didn't react when Braddock entered the room.

Though a native of Cuba, Captain Luis Garcia spoke good, if accented, English. Usually he told Braddock what to do, and the mate made it happen.

This conversation would be different.

"Captain, it's getting worse."

No reaction.

Was Braddock surprised? This time, though, he would just back off. He could see that Garcia's face also bore the telltale markings of the illness. The red rough patches, the peeling skin. The mate guessed that the captain must also feel that churning in his insides.

Braddock raised his voice.

"Captain, we have to *do* something."

Now, ever so slowly, Garcia turned to Braddock. Scattered among the rough patches, the captain's face was flecked with a wiry stubble. His eyes were narrow; the redness visible even here.

If they didn't act soon—Christ!—would there be any time at all?

"Do something?" The captain's face took on a sick grin. "Do *what*?"

"I told you. Everyone is sicker; soon you'll have no one to run the ship and—"

The captain laughed, a horrible laugh that degenerated into a hacking cough. He then spit right on the wheel-room floor. Braddock looked down; the sputum was flecked with blood.

"And what? Maybe some will die and then, guess what, *amigo*? More for you and me. That is unless you"—another sick grin—"die too!"

He's crazy, Braddock thought. Garcia had always been eccentric, a little wild; give him some cheap port and he could turn into a madman under the moon as the pearl ship stayed at anchor. Singing, laughing, until finally slipping into a Cuban patois that only one of the crew, one of the Cuban divers, understood.

That man was now below. Alive, but barely moving even when Braddock gave him a nudge.

"I don't want to die. None of us does, but if we keep going this way—"

The captain spun around in his chair and pointed a bony finger out to the sea. Braddock stared—how long since Garcia had a meal?

"Out there, straight ahead—hm?—are the Riau Islands. I will find a port. A place to land with our cargo,
a place to get well, a place—"

"No. We'll never get there. If we keep going this
way, we will all be dead well before then, Captain."

Garcia turned around and stared at Braddock.

Had he started to figure out what Braddock was
thinking, what the mate might do?

"So . . . what? You want to head for one of these
small islands? Someplace where, once they know what
we have below . . ." He repeated the words ". . . what
we have hidden below, they would just as soon kill us?"
Garcia nodded. "That's how we can die. Killed. Never
selling our prize, never getting any"—more coughs—
"help. No, there's only one thing we can do. Make for
the western islands."

"It's not the only thing we can do, Captain, we
can—"

But now Garcia had turned back to the sea. He
rested a scrawny hand on the wheel, almost as if the
wheel were steering him.

The conversation was over—for now.

Braddock nodded. He'd go down below and see how
the crew was doing. See, think . . . and plan.

Because, he imagined, none of them had any time at
all.

BOOK ONE
Before the Voyage
1932

1

Fortieth Street and Eighth Avenue,
New York City

ANN DARROW SAT ON THE hard wood chair—one of three—that faced the secretary's desk. The woman opposite her turned the pages of the *Daily News* while she chewed and popped her gum.

It was odd—as if Ann weren't even here. The wooden blinds sent slices of brilliant sun into the room and, at this angle, she could see thousands of tiny dust motes floating in the air.

Floating, she thought, *like me . . . loose, no direction.*
Maybe even a bit lost.

Her dream of being an actress, of having a career . . . it all seemed so fantastic now, almost impossible.

She looked at the office door. Every now and then she heard a laugh indicating that the meeting was still going on.

She had been waiting for thirty minutes . . . thirty minutes past her appointment. As if she didn't feel worthless enough.

Ann turned and looked at the door to the office, the beveled glass showing the backward letters that read

VICTOR MAJOR THEATRICALS. Then, below it, AGENTS TO THE STAGE AND SCREEN.

Screen.

That's where all the buzz was, Ann knew. Moving pictures kept getting bigger and bigger, and New York might not be the place to be anymore.

And what were her chances of getting to Hollywood, to act, to where this new world of movies was exploding despite the tough times?

None. Not without money.

And so far any money she earned was just barely enough to keep her going, pay the rent, pay for food.

She looked down at her shoes. Though she had polished them earlier, Ann saw that they still had scuff marks around the edges. New York was a tough town on shoes. And she had only two pair, and her others were showing even more signs of wear.

Her fingers held her hat tight. After her first check from the Follies, she had bought the hat. To treat herself. The style was *perfect*, and she loved how cute it looked. Though the curtain operator at those shows said, "Hey, Annie . . . looks like a helmet. You wanna nab a fella or go to war?"

Manny, her protector and the man who made her look so funny in their Follies act, said it was adorable.

Though it was a comic act, still it was . . . an act. An important step, she had thought.

If only the show had run longer . . .

Manny said something would turn up. *Irons in the fire,* he remarked.

There were always new shows, new productions, and always a new bunch of kids, singers, dancers, actors, waiting in the wings.

Waiting in the wings . . .

The secretary looked up in mid-chew. She didn't smile at Ann. *Guess I'm not a very high-ticket client*, she thought. Not even worth the occasional smile, or "Mr. Major will be right with you."

But then there was another burst of laughter, closer now, and the inner office door opened.

Victor Major, all four feet of him, came out, a chunky arm on the shoulder of someone easily a foot or two taller. That man, still grinning from whatever joke, looked down at Ann. A bold appraisal. *Another good-looking lug who thinks he's God's gift to women.*

Then Ann thought she recognized him. He starred in that new Cole Porter musical, *Gay Divorce*. Yeah, she had seen him.

The actor held the look for a moment as if asking, *Hey, doll, wanna walk out with me and twenty-three skidoo the meeting with your tubby agent?*

Ann turned away as the agent steered his client to the door.

"Right, right, well, you just keep those matinee ladies coming back for more, and 1932 will be a very good year."

The man turned to Major at the door. "I will do my very best. And you make sure you follow up with those film people."

Film. A fancy name for the photoplays. Fancier even than *movies. Film.* It's where Ann knew she should be, making people laugh.

"You got it, Roger. I'm watching out for you."

The two men shook hands, and then the dashing actor with the self-important smile left the room.

Major took a moment to stop—and adjust his demeanor.

All the smiles and heartiness vanished as if the agent had just stepped out of the shower into a suddenly bone-dry room.

"Okay, Ann. I guess we can talk, hm?"

Dripping with enthusiasm.

"Yes," she said.

And she stood up and followed the troll-like man into his office.

"You don't get it, kiddo. There isn't a lot out there."

Ann nodded. The agent seemed perpetually distracted by the Sargasso Sea of papers on his desk. Whatever the secretary did for the agent, it had nothing to do with organizing the mess in front of him.

"But," Ann began, "new shows are opening. All I need is to get into an audition. I'm good, and—"

Major looked over, a flicker of interest in his red-veined eyes. But not an interest in her talent, she immediately felt. The man smiled.

"Of course you're good, baby. I bet you are very good."

God, she thought. She thought she had dealt with

this when the agent first started handling her, when she was only eighteen. And now here it was again.

Maybe I sound too desperate.

This city, this country, was filled with desperate people. She hoped that maybe if Hoover lost the election, maybe change would come.

"But you know what," the agent went on, now opening a drawer, fiddling, digging as he spoke to her, "there are a ton of good kids out there, all of 'em wanting to act, on stage, on the big screen. It's called competition, and—ah—"

He pulled out a silver tube and slid out a half-smoked cigar.

If the agent had to save his half-spent stogie, then Ann guessed he wasn't exactly doing too well.

Major popped the cigar into his mouth and then lit a match. The room began to fill with the foul smoke.

"Competition," he continued through clenched teeth. "Though you know—there is something that might be great for you."

Ann smiled. She imagined that she was going to walk out of the room with nothing.

Major handed her a piece of paper. An audition at the Variety Playhouse—Ann guessed what that meant. Not a real show. Something passing for burlesque, with a good chance that some stripping was involved.

"I don't think—"

"Hey, don't be so fast. The Variety is doing a new show, wants some fresh . . . blood. It would just be something to tide you over. Until you got a real shot, know what I mean?"

She pushed the paper back. She knew other performers, young actresses and chorines who drifted into that, and further. Maybe hooking up with a sugar daddy and not calling it what it really was. A few, she heard, drifted into worse. Getting set up in apartments on the Upper East Side. All set up to run a little business, and then thoughts of acting slowly slipped away with the turnstile arrival of businessmen who still somehow managed to have money.

"No," she said. "I can't."

The agent shrugged. "That's a shame, sweetie. Wouldn't be bad. And I know a lot of other girls who'd jump at it." He looked right at her as he repeated the words . . . "Jump at it."

"No," she said again.

"Well, guess we're done here. Don't got nothing else. If I do, I'll give you a call—" He snapped his fingers, reinforcing his sarcasm. "Oh, forgot. You don't have a phone, do you?"

"The landlady can take a message."

"Right, sure. The landlady." He shook his head.

Ann leaned close. "You must have something else. Something real, doesn't matter what—or even where."

He took a puff and made a big smoke ring.

"Doesn't matter where? You're sure about that?"

"Absolutely."

"You know how to ride, don't you? Horses, I mean?"

Ann had spent her summers upstate . . . her mom

just dumping her off. And her grandfather made sure that she knew how to ride the small farm's two horses.

"Yes. I can."

For a moment Ann imagined some show with a Western theme, and they needed singers and dancers who could ride. She started to get excited. This could be something—

"And you . . . like to ride?"

Ann nodded, still excited, but now she noticed a funny smile on Major's face.

"Well—and you can relocate for a while. I mean, until something more substantial comes along?"

"Yes, I can, but—"

"Ever hear of the Steel Pier?"

The Steel Pier—a half-mile of shows, photoplays, exhibits—was a full day's entertainment for one low price. "Yes, I have. In Atlantic City."

"Yup. Good old AC. Greatest boardwalk in the world. The best salt water taffy too. And the seafood? Doesn't get fresher."

"But . . . what's the job?"

For a moment Ann forgot that they had started this by discussing her riding. She imagined that it might be something for an exhibit, a hostess, maybe talking about a new Ford, or—

"They need to add another girl to one of their big attractions. Maybe their biggest attraction."

The room now filled with a filmy smoke that started to make Ann feel sick.

I'm going to throw up if I don't get out of here.

"What will I do?"

"Something great, Ann. Something big. Probably biggest thing you'll ever do!"

She waited. The bastard loved that he was teasing her.

"You'll get on a horse, climb high above the crowds—and then dive right into the Atlantic Ocean! Now how about that?"

Ann looked out the window.

The world-famous diving horses of the Steel Pier.

And at least, she thought, *it isn't stripping. . . .*

2

SAM KELLY WATCHED THE AIR hose as it streamed into the murky water like an endless snake.

"I don't know why the hell they bother," DiGiacomo said. "I mean, what the hell for? This whole operation shuts down in what? Eight days. Eight goddamn days, and then this becomes just another abandoned Navy yard. I don't get it."

That DiGiacomo didn't get "it" was, by now, quite clear. The base was closing, and they were soon out of the Navy. What Sam also knew was that the short, barrel-chested diver didn't need any encouragement to continue. He was one of those special people who could continue a whole conversation, and keep it running all by himself.

Sam looked up.

He saw a small cruiser moored nearby, and a few Navy freight ships. To all appearances, this yard still looked like a going concern.

But he knew better.

His commission ended in three days; then the whole yard shuttered a week after that.

And yet . . . still the training continued. Young guys learning the ins and outs of hard-helmet diving, even though the U.S. Navy would be closing down shop here.

Then what?

Good question that.

For a Brooklyn boy, Sam had come far.

From the Irish ghetto of Flatbush to this near paradise of San Francisco. He remembered the first time he saw the pictures that fired his imagination, men in bulky dive suits and giant helmets, wandering through another world, stepping around coral and past schools of fish with amazing colors.

And sometimes the diver held a knife in his hand as a shark or barracuda did what—in the magazines at least—seemed natural . . . attack, teeth bared, ready to rip the tough material of the dive suit to shreds.

Yeah—as if that ever happened.

The few times Sam got close to a shark, no matter what size, it made a beeline in the other direction. And the so-called rays? That was the funniest.

In the pulp rags, the rays had some deadly "stinging" power. In truth they were gentle creatures with weird sucking mouthparts and not a real stinger in sight.

The air hose kept playing out.

The diver below, a kid named Tommy, was working the training wreck planted by the Navy, a rusty hulk that was used for all sorts of exercises. The kid was doing a "drop-in" . . . finding an access point to the interior of the ship, and then penetrating the wreck.

Just some practice.

"Yeah, so why the hell do they keep training all these kids, huh?" DiGiacomo asked.

His questions were never-ending.

Sam shook his head.

"Train them for what? The high-paying business of professional diving? Yeah. Gimme a break. We'll be lucky if we get a job selling chestnuts on Lombard Street." The lieutenant laughed, and jabbed a finger at Sam. "You just stay off my corner."

Sam looked at him. DiGiacomo's fear was transparent.

These were not good days to be cashiered out of a government job.

And what were Sam's prospects? He tried not to think too much about that. Unlike a lot of gobs, he had saved a decent nest egg. But how long would that last? What really were the opportunities in commercial diving? Did any of those opportunities still exist?

A lot of questions there.

A gull hovered over their barge, cawing at the generator pumping air. DiGiacomo had his hand around a tug line—the heavy rope used to signal that a diver was coming up.

The air hose stopped running out.

The line just . . . stopped, as it slipped into the water.

Sam turned to DiGiacomo. "Give the line a pull and see if everything's all right."

DiGiacomo gave the line a tug—and it flew back loose, sending him reeling to the floor of the barge.

"Christ, it broke."

Sam gave the air hose a tug now. Taut, and the air compressor was still chugging so that the kid below, Tommy Hautala, had to be breathing okay, the valve venting.

"Shit," Sam said, standing up, peering into the water as if it would tell him what was wrong.

"Something's up, Sam. Something's going on down there."

Right, Sam thought. *Something's going on and we don't have a clue what it is.*

"I gotta go down," Sam said.

"Damn. Maybe you should give him a bit more time."

Sam turned to DiGiacomo, knowing what he was thinking. They both had just a few days until they were done. It was not a time to take any risks, any chances. Maybe they could wait, give the kid some time to figure out his problem.

Sure. They could wait. But if the kid was in trouble, they might be bringing up a corpse.

Not the way Sam wanted to end his Navy service.

He ran over to a dive suit hanging on a pole.

"Jeezus, Sam? What the hell you doin'?"

"I'm suiting up. Give me a hand."

"But by the time you get down there, the kid—"

Sam reached out and grabbed DiGiacomo's wrists. Not the time for him to be spouting off. "Just help me suit up, okay?"

DiGiacomo nodded.

And though Sam went as fast as possible, slipping into the bulky dive outfit, the heavy metal boots, it still took minutes, precious minutes that if Tommy was in real trouble could make Sam too late.

Finally DiGiacomo went and grabbed the helmet and hooked it to a second air hose. The compressor would now feed two lifelines below.

"All set, Sam?"

Sam nodded, and DiGiacomo put the helmet over Sam's head, pressing it tight, then twisting it so the large glass porthole of the helmet faced forward.

"Hurry up, DiGiacomo."

"I'm hurrying, I'm hurrying!"

DiGiacomo took a wrench and tightened the bolts around the helmet. Then he tapped the top of the helmet.

"All set, Sam?"

Sam nodded. The suit was unbearably heavy on the surface. The lead shoes made walking almost impossible, and the helmet made it hard to keep his head erect. The only solution was getting into the water as fast as possible.

Sam stepped to an opening in the port side of the barge. He turned back to make sure that his partner was ready to play out the air hose.

Most dives got screwed up in those first few seconds of hitting the water, the hose tangling as the diver fell like a deadweight to the bottom.

Sam took a giant step into the water, the surface of San Francisco Bay glistening in the midday sun.

*   *   *

And he fell . . .

The bottom lay at only about sixty feet deep here. Not much of a dive. But the visibility, always bad, made the harbor one of Sam's least favorite places to be underwater. Get out into the Pacific, and there the water quickly cleared to thirty, forty . . . even fifty feet visibility.

Here, he could see five, ten feet if he was lucky.

And as soon as he hit the silty bottom, he knew this wasn't one of the bay's better days.

The visibility might even be less than five feet. Finding the wreck, and then finding the kid, wasn't going to be easy.

Sam began walking in the direction of the wreck, leading with his head, tilting forward to allow for movement on the bottom. People were already working on other ways of diving, free of the bulky suit, the lead boots, the heavy metal collar and helmet.

But until those ways were perfected, this was all they had.

He moved quickly but with an awareness that the wreck could appear in front of him, out of the gloom, so suddenly. He felt his right boot step onto . . . something, and for a moment he lost his balance. The bottom was littered with everything from whiskey bottles to chunks of discarded furniture. A veritable dumping ground.

He steadied himself, and looked ahead.

Then—he saw the wreck, a small freighter used for training, with great gashes in its side and a deck stripped of anything valuable.

He looked around for a sign of the other air hose, or bubbles escaping to the surface.

But with the visibility so poor, he couldn't see anything.

Which way to go? It was potluck at this point. Pick one direction to circle the wreck, or the other. No matter. And every minute could be bringing bigger problems to the young diver.

Sam took a deep breath, the compressed air with a dry, metallic taste. He licked his lips—a bit of moisture—but it didn't do much good.

He moved right, surging forward, head leading, going around the rusting freighter. Every step made a few more feet of the hull appear in the gloom.

Come on, he thought. *Where the hell are you?* All the kid was supposed to do was find an opening, enter, take a look around, and then get out.

Where the hell was—

Sam stopped. He saw the air hose trailing into the wreck, a thick fat tube of life snaking into the hulk. Saw bubbles escaping.

Could be this is my lucky day, Sam thought. *Could be the kid is okay, just had a bit of trouble inside.* The lifeline cut by some rust metal, but the thick air hose working fine. Take something seriously sharp to cut through that.

Far more common for an air hose to get pinched, bent, and then cut the diver off from air.

But with the bubbles escaping to the surface, this all looked okay.

Sam trudged closer to the dark hole that the kid had selected for his jump into the wreck. Black, shadowy, hiding everything for now, but about to reveal just what was going on with the young diver.

He grabbed his own tug line and gave it three strong yanks . . . meaning that he was okay down here.

Okay for now.

And maybe coming back up soon.

What every diver hoped.

Back up soon, for some laughs, some diving tales, a cold beer or two.

Yeah. A nice image to hold.

Sam moved to the wreck and the open gash.

3

Latitude 65, Longitude 65—
Off the coast of Baffin Island, Canada
THE *VENTURE* ROCKED, AND Carl Denham grabbed the
railing even as he felt breakfast begin a nearly complete
trip up his gorge and onto the soaked deck. He pulled
and tightened the fur collar of his coat.

The captain, Englehorn, seemed somehow magically
stable, as if he had powerful magnets that kept him
firmly planted on the deck. Denham, on the other
hand, felt as if each swell were a bucking bronco ready
to throw him over the side.

"Damn, Englehorn, I've sailed a lot, but is the sea
always like this?"

The captain laughed and took a big puff on his pipe.
Then he turned to Denham. "It's the North Atlantic, Mr.
Denham, in winter. Besides dodging the ice floes, you got
swells and currents that can treat this ship like a toy."

Denham looked out to the ocean. He saw those
swells, crazy dips in the sea that rocked back and forth,
intersecting, overlapping, sometimes sending up a
choppy plume of white water that he imagined was
taller than the ship itself.

"Right. I knew that. Just want to be sure this is all okay, all normal."

Another puff. "Oh, it's normal, all right. Normal bad. At least we're heading south. Might get a little better the closer we get to Nova Scotia."

The boat took another mad ride up one wave, sliding down another, before—Denham could clearly see—the *Venture* became sandwiched between two giant swells that seemed ready to make the small freighter into a pancake.

"God," Denham said.

"No God here, Denham. Just the sea, doing what it's always done."

The two swells hit, and a shower of icy water went flying over the deck. Denham saw the captain pull his cap down, then look up at the boathouse. Hayes was at the wheel.

"Hayes okay?" Denham asked.

"Okay? That man has a Crois de Guerre, won in battle. This wouldn't rattle him. Me, I'm getting too old for this."

The *Venture* tilted left and right, bobbing so low that Denham thought that it might let the sea rush onto the deck, and down to the cabins.

"You know, Denham, you can go below. Though I bet they're feeling a lot worse than you are. I've already heard Lumpy screaming about the kitchen. Apparently tonight's stew is all over. Guess it will be yesterday's biscuits and some canned beans."

"Maybe we should heave to, lay anchor, or whatever

the terminology is, Englehorn? Can't there be hidden rocky outcrops out here—I sure wouldn't want to abandon ship in this sea."

Another laugh from Englehorn, who, Denham realized, was clearly enjoying this.

"As for any exposed outcrops, that's why they invented charts. We know where we're going."

For a moment, Denham considered going down below. Get out of the icy air, away from the crazy spray of sea water, the endless rolling and bobbing. But then—imagining the close quarters, the smell—he realized as nasty as it was on deck, it had to be better.

And, he also thought . . . *we're heading south, back to New York—and we don't have what we came for.*

There were implications to that last statement.

Most of them financial.

Zelman backed this little expedition because Denham had promised—*promised*—to deliver something amazing. He was so good at pitching, so good at creating the image of what was going to be on the silver screen.

Imagine . . . he told them . . . *footage of an animal at once real and mythic, an animal that dwarfs any shark ever seen, a sea creature capable of swallowing a seal in a single gulp. I'll bring back amazing footage . . . and the story of the killer whale, the orca.*

But not just any orca, not just any killer whale. Denham had spoken to some of the fishermen out of Prince Edward Island who had run as far north as Baffin Island. They told him of seeing an orca that truly deserved the name *killer*. All fishermen exaggerate, but even if it was just an ancient whale feeding in the seal-rich waters, it would still be incredible.

And if not, if he didn't find this mythic orca?

Then he'd still have great footage of schools of the sharklike whales, that and some of the natives, the local Inuit, their lives fading ever since the days Flaherty filmed his *Nanook*.

By the time Denham finished pitching, the backers felt more than confident in bankrolling Denham's' cinematographic expedition to the north.

And now?

No orcas at all. Lots of seal, even some whales—all good footage, but not what he promised. Englehorn suggested that the killer whales might have gone south.

"They follow the food, Denham. Just like the Eskimo. Follow the food, hunt. Could be—they're not here."

That's what Englehorn said, but Denham wondered if the steely-eyed captain just wanted to get the hell out of the sea. The *Venture* was better suited to the calmer waters of the tropics. And Englehorn didn't want to risk losing his ship just to get Denham some great footage.

"I wouldn't mind," Englehorn said as the vessel rose the crest of another massive swell, "finding a place to lay anchor. We'll need some shelter though or it could be worse than chugging through this mess."

"Sounds good to me."

"Let me talk to Hayes, look at the charts, and maybe"—he clapped Denham on the back—"bring you some relief, hm?"

"Great."

Denham watched Englehorn turn and bolt up a ladder to the wheel room, moving deftly despite the rocking of the ship.

And Denham returned to staring at the battling waves, as he rose up and down on the balls of his toes, trying to second-guess the erratic pattern as the ship bobbed and weaved through the stormy North Atlantic.

4

San Francisco Bay

SAM TURNED AROUND AND CHECKED his air hose. It streamed down from the surface and there didn't seem to be anything to catch it.

At least, nothing for it to snag on out here.

Inside the wreck would be a different story.

He looked at the other air hose leading into the gaping hole. If the kid Tommy was in real trouble, then they would know topside. Once a diver stopped breathing and venting air from the suit, it became quite clear up there that a problem had arisen.

So if the kid was in danger, at least he was still breathing.

Sam reached out and grabbed a jagged edge of the opening. This freighter wreck had been used by the dive teams for more than five years, getting rustier, the oxidized iron hull turning nastier, sharper.

Good thing they were closing this down before someone gets hurt.

That is . . . if someone hadn't gotten hurt already.

He pushed into the opening, and immediately whatever little light and visibility there was vanished.

Sam turned on the lamp attached to his belt. The batteries for the diving lights were heavy; rumor had it that there were some new types of lights being developed. But for now, he had to make do with a bulky light.

Which is when he got worried.

The other diver's light should be on.

Should be. He should see the glow of Tommy's light inside the hull.

Instead—nothing. Unless the trainee went in deep, turned a corner. He was supposed to just drop into the wreck for a look-see.

That's all. But did curiosity get the better of him? That, or confusion?

Confusion. A diver's worst enemy. You look around for where you came from, and then head in exactly the wrong direction. Maybe you cross over your air tube and start to panic.

Confusion, panic, then you're looking at making lots of mistakes.

And with enough mistakes, you're dead.

It was as simple as that.

Sam felt three tugs on his lifeline. He reached for it and gave three tugs back.

All okay down here.

That is, if you didn't count the fact that the other diver had gone too deep.

Sam took another step. The pale yellow light picked up the outline of a bulkhead corridor. He knew that it led down a staircase leading to the bridge, and past the radio room and a small mess.

He looked down there, and saw the other air hose trailing in, then vanishing in the gloom. Even with the light, he couldn't see more than ten feet.

But the diver was down here.

Did Tommy get confused, curious?

And was he now in trouble?

That was the other thing; a diver in trouble was bad news. Try to rescue him, and it could turn into a panicked tussle, with shoes and lines tangling, until it became a trap for two.

The two divers with their helmets close together, eyes wide with fear, realizing that they were now both looking at death.

Sam reached out to the walls of the corridor to steady himself, and took a step forward.

Only a few steps, still leading with his head for balance, hands to the side to steady himself—and Sam saw the glow.

Right, Tommy's light had to be getting weak. The batteries were crap; they just didn't last long enough. The glow turned a sick yellow. But it told him that the diver was in the room to the right, the radio room.

Sam tried to form a quick mental picture of it. Tall shelves with radio equipment. A long table, two chairs. Not the worst room to stumble into. Except for all that shelving.

Not that sturdy, and probably had been loosened from the wall. Lots of exposed metal, jagged metal that rusted a bit more each week.

Why did Tommy go in there?

Sam took another few steps and then reached the entrance.

He turned slowly. When you wore so much weight with the helmet, the lead yoke around your neck, the damn shoes, you had to move at a snail's pace to avoid the sheer weight of the suit sending you flying.

He saw the kid.

Shit . . .

Sam's brighter light picked up the outline of the diver, the shelves, the furniture—and what had probably happened.

5

Off the coast of Baffin Island

DENHAM FELT THE *VENTURE* START to turn, heading into the waves. Now the small freighter plowed into the massive swells, riding up and down. He could only imagine what it was like belowdecks.

The crew hadn't been too happy before; you just never lost that bone-chilling cold soaked into your bones. That they blamed Denham was clear to the director. He started shrugging off their looks, though he did overhear two crewmen asking when the hell they'd be heading south.

South.

Back to the relative warmth of New York City. The sailors had a relatively short memory. Some of them had been on the streets till they had been recruited by Englehorn for this trip. Hard times in the US of A—and a job in the freezing Arctic had to be better than starving in the gutters of New York, or maybe living in a Hooverville shack of cardboard. At least here they had a bunk, and what passed as food from Lumpy's mess.

They should be grateful. . . .

But being out here changed things. Englehorn seemed unflappable. He just kept smoking his pipe, looking at the weather, complaining about the promised appearances of schools of orcas . . . that never materialized.

And not for the first time Carl Denham had to wonder . . . *What the hell am I doing?*

It was one thing to lead a film crew and actors into the rain forest of British Honduras looking for giant constrictors (and *finding* them, damn it!). Or his trip to the Congo searching for the lost elephant graveyard. And well, not finding that one, but still coming back with incredible footage, and even a few credible performances.

And that's what it used to be about— the footage! Characters facing amazing things never seen before, things that only Carl Denham could deliver.

But was that enough anymore?

His friend Jack might be right.

Maybe . . . Denham needed a better story, better actors.

Which meant—a writer!

And that was the other thing about this trip, another difference.

They returned from Central America not only with a great picture, but with a cargo full of wild animals. The zoos of the world tried to outbid one another, especially for some of the exotic snakes that they brought back. Englehorn was a good captain—but he was *great* at wrangling animals.

And even though the young creatures didn't survive the trip back from the Congo, still the Africa movie turned a profit even before Denham sold the picture to Joe Kennedy's outfit.

Apparently, he liked the young starlet Denham used.

But now, the big studios didn't want Denham's stuff. Now he dealt with smaller outfits, with money men who didn't care what kind of film they showed.

So this—despite the sick rise and fall of the ship—was where he belonged. In the world, looking for the incredible place to tell an incredible story.

The *Venture* smashed down into a watery valley and Denham grabbed the railing.

Could be this was getting seriously dangerous.

In which case he really should try to get below.

But getting below meant making his way twenty feet or so to the entranceway, while all the while the ship jerked up and down.

Twenty feet, with no railing.

The ship rose up again, and Denham turned to see the stern nearly disappear in the trough, the white froth atop the gray sea looking as though it was grabbing for the ship.

This isn't good, Carl thought. No matter how competent a captain Englehorn was, this just was looking bad.

The ship began another plunge forward, into the trough of yet another swell.

Denham's stomach heaved yet again—even though it was empty.

San Francisco Bay

Sam stopped and let his light play on the scene. Tommy had obviously gone in, attracted by the water-logged radio equipment, all so ancient. Maybe he touched something, or grabbed a shelf for support.

Something gave—perhaps a bolt holding a shelf to a wall.

And one tall shelf shifted, pinning the kid. Pinning him, but he was damn lucky that nothing happened to his air hose.

Finally Sam let his light fall on the kid's faceplate. The other diver's eyes looked as if they were set to bug out of his head.

But he was alive; air still pumped into the helmet.

Sam held up a hand, and made a patting gesture in the water.

Nice and easy. Steady. Calm.

Easier said than done when you're sixty feet down, and pinned inside a small room. Was the kid panicked? Hard to tell, but Sam had to be ready for the possibility that as he got close, Tommy might do something stupid.

Sam looked at his own lifeline. DiGiacomo would be expecting some tugs signaling that all was okay.

Not a good idea. Not now, when the rope snaked into the hull, past rusty jagged bits of the hull and exposed metal of the bulkheads. The rope could easily get cut, and then DiGiacomo would think that Sam was in trouble.

Another diver down, another rescue mission.

No, better he let DiGiacomo think that he just forgot.

He took a step closer to Tommy. A small cloud of muck flew up from his feet. The cloud rose then swirled around the room, caught by some current that snaked its way through the wreck.

Three days left in the Navy, and I got this, Sam thought. It's like the guys he spoke to who were in the Great War . . . and how they saw their buddies buy the farm just days before the whole thing ended, days before they were due to be sent home.

Moving close, Sam saw that the shelf looked as though it had slipped away from the wall and swung into the diver. The suit looked uncut . . . a good thing. But the weight obviously had Tommy pinned.

No time for anything fancy, no time to go back up and get some tools.

Sam would have to move it as best he could and hope that Tommy could help.

Though the possibility was equally strong that he could make things worse.

And for a second, Sam had a quick flashback. He was back in Sheepshead Bay, back on the Brooklyn dock as the fishing boats came in. And with a few of his friends . . . he dived for nickels thrown by people into the unbelievably murky water.

Once he went down, chasing a nickel spiraling away, catching it just as it nearly hit the bottom—but then feeling something *catch him*.

Some bit of wood, maybe an old chunk of dock, an old mooring pole with a big nail head sticking out. A nail head that just caught his swimsuit, holding him.

That amazing rush of panic.

Suddenly aware that all the air you have is what you hold in your lungs, your last breath, just before you dived.

That awareness making the desire to breathe irresistible.

Reaching behind, then around, feeling for where his suit was caught, finally feeling the metal trap, the chunk of nail now dug into the suit.

More precious moments, and then the desire to breathe becoming a fire in his lungs.

Beginning to pray. Back then, a kid in Brooklyn, he prayed a lot.

Prayed for everything.

Finally, tugging the material of the suit, feeling it move, then, finally, slip off the nail head.

Racing to the surface.

To the taunts, the laughs, the question—did you get it?

Did you get the nickel?

Not telling them that in his moment of terror the prized nickel was, of course, let go, released, lost forever in the muck.

He pretended that everything was fine when he climbed out.

You didn't talk about fear, not with your friends.

But Sam knew how powerful it was, and if Tommy lost it, they could both end up dying down here.

Another heavy step, another mucky cloud, and now Sam reached for the metal structure of the shelving for the first time. . . .

6

Baffin Island

SUDDENLY THE *VENTURE* TURNED INTO a small bay made by twin spits of rock, and the mad roller-coaster ride just as quickly calmed. The boat still rocked back and forth, but it didn't feel like each eddy of the sea could break over the bow and try to bring the ship down.

And that's a good thing, Denham thought.

Yeah, let the storm settle, then figure out where the hell they could go.

Looking for the elusive killer whales.

What is it with me and elusive things? Denham thought. Nice kid from Sturbridge Village, a little bit of college, then—something happened. Small-town America had proved too small for him. He liked being out here, the world full of surprises, danger, excitement. And who knows what hasn't been discovered yet?

. . . But how long would they remain undiscovered before everything was found that could be found? No more hidden treasure, no lost graves, no creatures never seen before. The clock was ticking, and Denham knew, as best as he could understand it himself, that he wanted to be one of those people who found those things, capture them on film, and showed the world . . . before the well completely dried up.

He looked up, and the *Venture* kept chugging into the small bay. He saw outcrops sending up water, warning signs that rocky traps lay hidden under the foam.

The engines of the *Venture* slowed. Denham looked up to the wheelhouse, and saw the silhouette of Engle-horn, pointing at the shore.

Then back to the water, as they passed an outcrop only about twelve feet away.

Denham thought: *Maybe we should stop right here, drop anchor. Would be a nasty place to take a gash to the hull.*

Then the door from belowdecks opened, and some of the crew spilled out scrambling, racing. The engines stopped, and the fore and aft anchors, both fastened to a heavy metal chain, began running to the bottom.

Denham looked back to the rocks. A few good swells, and an unanchored *Venture* could easily be thrown against them.

But then a voice—Hayes.

"Captain! Aft anchor secure."

Then, from the front, one of the other crew: "Fore anchor down, Captain, and holding." And Denham could feel it. The ship held, pinned from both front and back, locked in place. There was still enough give in the placement of the anchors that the ship wobbled some in the churning sea. But she didn't really move; she'd take no gashes to her hull today.

Nice to know, Denham thought.

And now, for the first time, he looked up from the roiling sea, from the minelike rocks dotting the bay, up even from the rock-strewn shore to see:

Low-lying hills, and a small snow-covered valley cutting through them, and then, in the distance:

Smoke. Three, maybe four thin plumes of whitish smoke rising straight into the air, like thin bony fingers up to the steel gray sky.

People. On this godforsaken, barren piece of rock.

Fortune. Fate. Call it what you will, things always turn up for me, thought Denham. *Something always happens.*

The world is a big place, full of big surprises.

And there are only so many people like me to take advantage of them.

Preston had come out of the depths of the ship, looking green. Must have been a bad hour for Denham's assistant, puking up his guts in the closed quarters below.

"Suck in some air, Preston. Looks like you need it."

Preston nodded and then leaned over the side and barked at the water, though, Denham could see, his stomach was thankfully empty.

"Maybe you need something more than some nice clean air, hm?"

Finally Preston stood up, nearly cross-eyed.

"A little shaky, Preston? Should have rid out the storm topside. Best way to deal with weather like that."

His assistant nodded without too much enthusiasm.

"Anyway, my man—look over there!"

Denham pointed at the smoke. Preston was barely able to lift his head.

"Some people somewhere. Eskimo, I imagine. How long has it been since Flaherty's *Nanook*? What do we know about these amazing people? Their lives, their survival—and the animals they hunt, eat, wear. Fortune just gave us a gift, Preston. A new wrinkle for our story. What's that expression, fortune favors the prepared?"

"What—what if," Preston could barely burble out the word, "they don't want us filming them. Remember that tribe near Guatemala?"

"That turned out okay."

"Okay, because we had enough guns to make them think twice about cutting our heads off."

"Right. No one lost their heads. And Eskimo? Everything we know about them tells us they welcome visitors. We'll bring some stuff to trade, some food, biscuits, cookies, maybe some of Lumpy's canned meat. You better tell Baxter we'll be adding to his role."

"He looks greener than me. And you want to give them some of Lumpy's food? How will they open the cans, Carl?"

"See, you always look for the problems. I see solutions. Opportunity. That, out there, is an opportunity. Why don't you tell Herb we're going to want the camera soon, and get Mike moving too—I'm gonna want sound for this."

"Now?"

Denham rolled his eyes. "Yes, now. We still have hours of daylight."

Preston nodded at the wheelhouse. "And Englehorn is okay with this?"

"Englehorn works for me, right? Besides, he sure doesn't want to get back to the open sea yet. So this is perfect. Hey, maybe we'll stay for a few days. I'll go get things moving, you see Herb and Mike."

Denham started up to the wheelhouse, already planning how he would lay out this little shore expedition for Englehorn.

A last glance at the smoke, and he had to hope that those telltale plumes didn't vanish before he hit the rocky beach with his shore party.

San Francisco Bay

One yank, and the shelving didn't budge.

Sam felt Tommy's hand on his wrist, and Sam turned to look at the pinned diver's face. The kid looked scared. He said something, barely audible through the thick glass and incessant bubbles of the compressor feeding him air, the release valve sending a noisy air exhaust to the surface.

But Sam could make out the two words on the second try.

"It . . . hurts!"

Hurts. Sam knew the kid was trapped, but if he was hurt there was something else going on here that he hadn't seen. He tilted his head up and down, searching Tommy's suit. Up, down, scanning the suit. Sam could see one shelf edge pressed tight against the kid's chest—that was the one Sam was about to move. But could that really hurt Tommy? Maybe he was exaggerating?

Then he saw it.

A metal bar from a lower shelf, a bit of jagged metal that must have jutted out when the shelving moved—stuck right into the kid's side. Sam kept his light on the metal, where it hit the heavy material of the dive suit. These suits could resist the razor sharpness of coral, twisted spires of coral that could cut a man's flesh with just a casual scrape.

But this sharp metal had sliced into Tommy's suit.

The suit was indented, the metal pressing into the boy's body just above the hip.

Christ, that had *to hurt.*

Suddenly Sam had new respect for the kid. Trapped down here, in this eight-foot-by-eight-foot watery tomb, and the constant pressure, the pain of that metal bar. Sam brought his head and his lamp up to the kid's faceplate, and gave him a thumbs-up.

Okay. It's okay, kid, I see the problem, you can stop worrying now.

But that was bullshit. Sam didn't see an easy way out of this. In fact, for the first time he thought that maybe he would have to go back up, get tools, something to cut away the metal.

And all the time the kid's nitrogen debt was building. He had already been down here too long, breathing air at this depth for too long. Getting to the surface would bring an even deadlier bout of the bends.

As it was, Sam would have to take it nice and easy getting Tommy back up.

Nice and easy.

Like now. Nice and easy—the way he'd have to free him.

Carefully, like some palsied old man, Sam struggled to kneel on the cabin floor. His padded knees hit the floor and set up cloudy swirls. He waited a second until the visibility cleared a bit, then leaned close, his helmet now only inches away from where the metal spar jutted into Tommy.

Sam saw he was wrong.

The metal had begun to tear the tough material of the suit. He couldn't be sure, but Sam imagined that the metal jutted into the midsection of the other diver.

No blood yet.

Let's be glad we're not doing this off Hawaii. Wounded diver, blood, and you're looking at sharks. And with the lousy mobility of the dive suit, the shark could play with a diver like a toy, twisting, turning, getting his air hose and life line tangled, until ready to try a big bite.

Let's be thankful.

Sam didn't pray. His brief days as an altar boy at St. Vinnie's were a long time ago. But now, the thought passed his mind. *Give me a hand here.*

Because this is not good.

He reached for the metal spar. He heard a yelp from inside Tommy's helmet.

Right, that hurts. I know that. Sam didn't look up at the kid. What he had to do was best done without the burning image of the bug-eyed kid staring at Sam, pleading.

Sam felt the kid lay a heavily gloved hand on his shoulder, begging, pleading that he be careful.

But there was no easy way to do this.

Not with the time pressure, not with the nitro buildup. Not in this cramped hellhole on what Sam knew had to be his last dive here for the good old U.S. Navy.

He put his other hand on the metal spar. He grabbed hard.

He looked at the twisted shelving, only inches away, to make sure that he wasn't missing anything, some detail of the trap that he might be missing.

He had all the information he was going to get.

His grip tightened.

He was ready.

7

THE CAB WENT DOWN CONNECTICUT Avenue and then stopped before the boardwalk.

The day had started in Manhattan, sunny, hopeful—but as soon as she got into the Greyhound bus for Atlantic City, she could see the clouds. Rolling in, thickening, until now it was a dark gray overhead.

Great day at the beach, she thought.

She saw a few people walking down a wooden ramp from the boardwalk, and a few others walked directly off the beach onto the street.

Nothing like clouds and the threat of rain and lightning to scare people away from the ocean.

"So here you are, dollface. You sure you wanna get out? Looks nasty. Maybe you could use a bite—or something?"

The cabbie had his cap tipped back, giving his face the same weird grinning look of a ventriloquist's dummy. She once worked with a dummy, actually the dummy and its owner. Sir Charles and Elmer, the act was called. The guy wasn't much of a ventriloquist, and the jokes were even worse. Ann got most of the laughs flirting with the dummy.

Now *that* was acting.

But she hated the way the dummy looked. Glassy eyes with lids that blinked like a meat chopper falling down.

She asked "Sir" Charles once: *What's the deal with the red lips on the dummy?*

"Why, my dear Ann, that way the rubes can see his lips move and, with luck, not see mine."

Though they did see, much more noticeably during the later shows, until it seemed as if Sir Charles, who affected the air of an aristocrat with this rude dummy for a friend, didn't seem to care anymore.

Creepy. Dummies, clowns—the bottom rungs of show business.

And maybe . . . this.

But Ann thought that if now she was about to experience something close to the bottom of show business, it was still *legit* show business at least.

"No. I'll get out here."

The driver shook his head. By now a few drops of rain started hitting the windshield. "I dunno sweetheart, raining and all. And you wanna get out?"

"How much?" she said.

The driver's eyes widened a bit, and she wondered if he had yet another gambit to throw her way.

"I'm in a rush."

He laughed. "You missed the sun, lady. But it's sixty-five cents. Without the tip, of course."

Ann had to watch every penny, as if they could steal

off on their own. She needed this job, and she needed to make it work. Get ahead a little bit, save some money. Then back to New York and try again. The bad days on Broadway couldn't last forever. Get rid of Hoover, and things had to get better.

Wouldn't they?

She gave him the coins, with a ten-cent tip.

"Last of the big-time—" the man started to say, but Ann already was out the door, out on the street, slamming the door on the dummy-faced cabdriver.

Should have given him nothing.

Stupid man.

She walked quickly, and directly up the ramp, stepping onto the splintery wood that led to the main boardwalk.

People moved quickly up here, hurrying one way or the other. She did see some people hanging at stands, gobbling corn on the cob, or shoveling down wieners dripping mustard and sauerkraut. Small overhangs protecting them when the storm finally came.

She had to find this place, the famous Steel Pier, before the rain came down.

But that wasn't hard to do.

About another block down, she saw a massive sign filled with hundreds of lights for the nighttime. Giant letters proclaiming STEEL PIER.

Is it really of steel, she wondered? *Why would you make a pier out of steel? Wouldn't wood be better? Or was that just dumb?*

As she hurried to it, she could see how big it was—a mammoth pier jutting into the Atlantic, the sea now filled with foamy white rolling waves, the water an ominous dark gray just like the sky.

Good thing I'm not superstitious, Ann thought.

She felt the first drops of water hit her arms. She wore her cute hat that she really shouldn't have bought, shaped like a cup, a creamy tan color. She loved it—but getting it soaked wouldn't be good.

Close to the entrance, she watched people stream out of the pier. Wasn't it an indoor place with shows, movies? Why wouldn't people stay?

She started to fight her way past the surging crowd.

But then a man in a blue uniform who looked like a conductor stepped in front of her.

"I'm sorry, miss. They're closing the pier for the day. A bad storm coming in. They don't want their patrons—"

"I'm—I'm not a patron. I'm here to—"

The man held his hand up to some other now-wet stragglers who were trying to head into the pier.

Ann dug into her purse and pulled out a piece of paper.

"I'm supposed to meet this man, Mr. Jerome Nadler."

The guard raised his eyes. "Mr. Nadler, hm?" He took the piece of paper.

"He's interviewing me for a job. I'm to dive, with the horses. I'm a rider, I guess they—"

The guard waved the piece of paper at her. "You

sure Mr. Nadler knows you're coming? I'm not even sure he's here today. He usually comes by for lunch, then off to his club, or—"

"Please. I've come a long way. New York City. It's starting to pour out."

"And worse on the way, it looks like."

"Right. So if I could just keep my appointment with him, that would be great."

The man smoothed his black mustache flecked with gray.

"Okay, then. Guess it's okay. But you best check in with the ticket office. They can ring him. See if he's there. Let him know you're coming."

Impulsively Ann reached out and gave the man's arm a squeeze.

"Thank you. Thank you so much."

The man nodded and smiled. "Let's hope Mr. Nadler doesn't have you trying the horses today, eh? They get spooked when the sea gets choppy, and it's gone way beyond choppy."

Another squeeze, and Ann headed in the direction of the ticket booth.

"Yes, sir, I will tell the young lady to go right in."

The man in the ticket booth hung up the phone and gave Ann a ticket.

"Show this to the people inside."

Ann looked down to see a ticket that read: *Visitor's Pass—The Steel Pier.*

"And where should I go?"

"Oh, okay. Once you're in, just follow the signs, past the theaters, past the food display and big ballroom. That's where you'll head, got it, sister?"

"Out to where they have the water show, the horses?"

The man squinted a bit behind his glasses. "No, not out there. Nobody out there now. That's all closed up. No, Mr. Nadler will meet you by the bell."

Ann opened her mouth, as if about to ask a question. But she had that first slight hesitation, as if things might not be what she thought them to be.

"The bell?"

The man nodded again even as he took some bills out of a drawer and began counting them. So many bills—hard to imagine that people still came here, that some people still had money to spend. She noticed the sign above the ticket booth's cage. ONE LOW PRICE—SEE ALL THE SHOWS!

"Yup, the bell," he said again.

Finally she had to ask the question.

"What bell?"

The man shook his head, looking as if he was thinking . . . didn't everyone know this? Was Ann somehow left off the list of people who . . . knew this?

"The diving bell, girlie. The Steel Pier's diving bell. That's where Mr. Nadler is going to meet you. And you better hurry. I hear he hates to be kept waiting."

He went back to counting his money, so Ann pulled back.

She was clueless as to why they'd meet there.

Did Mr. Nadler have an office there?

Another step backward, and the man looked up as if noting her lack of progress.

And then Ann turned, and started hurrying into the mammoth interior of America's showplace, inside the pier filled with stage shows, and cars, and exhibits, and movies, and—apparently—something called a diving bell.

8

San Francisco Bay

SAM CHECKED TOMMY'S EXHAUST VALVE. Everything seemed okay with the kid—except for his bug-eyed look staring out of the round porthole.

Come on, Sam thought. *Just don't panic.*

Don't go all crazy, grab me, get us both trapped down here. I'm almost done with this job.

Let me get out alive.

Sam tugged on the metal spar pinning the other diver. It didn't budge—in fact, it seemed like it never could have moved, the big chunk of metal rammed into the kid's midsection.

Sam raised his hands up to Tommy, palms out, signaling *Hold on. We're okay here.*

Though Sam had the thought that we're definitely not okay. The kid had been down way too long, that metal close to ripping into his suit. Tommy's light was just about dead, down to a pathetic yellow that barely illuminated the bits of debris swirling around his helmet.

And my light won't last forever either, Sam knew.

He looked around the rooms reaching for . . . something.

There, in the corner, was what looked like a loose bit of metal. Maybe it had popped off when the shelving moved.

Sam took a heavy step forward, and another, and then reached out for the metal. His gloved hand closed around it, felt its weight. A nice piece of steel.

He turned back to Tommy. Bad news.

Small bubbles escaping from his suit where the spear was.

If this found piece of metal helped, if Sam actually could use it to free the other diver, the kid would have a hole in his suit. Small now, but damned sure to get bigger.

Sam hesitated.

It was this moment they talked about when he trained in New London. Toward the very end of the advanced instruction—advanced in the sense you had a master chief talking and acting like he'd seen anything and everything under the sea.

He told some stories . . . diving a wreck off Block Island, a recovery. Real seas, not a practice in a calm bay. And a diver gets trapped in a corridor when a bulkhead shifts.

There may come that moment, he said, *when you know that it's over for the other guy. And you have to know . . .*

Here the chief raised his voice and looked at the roomful of now supposedly advanced helmet divers: *And you have to know that it's over for him.*

The message was clear. There could come a time when you had to protect your own skin. Get the hell out of there, and be glad that it was, maybe, the other guy this time, and not you.

Sam looked at Tommy. The eyes showed fear, but now maybe something else. The kid wasn't stupid. Resignation.

Was it that time yet? Sam wondered.

Time to let him go?

Hell no, he thought.

He came closer to Tommy.

Sam didn't make eye contact. *No, let it look as though I'm just doing what has to be done. . . .*

Besides, Sam didn't need to see those same wild eyes. He quickly wedged the metal piece under the bar pinning the trapped diver. He levered it up slowly until metal touched metal, using part of the shelf as a resistance point.

Sam's light had faded a bit. Now the murky shadows in the underwater room deepened. He could barely make out the outline of the two pieces of metal, the shelving, the place where one piece dug into Tommy's suit.

The angle looked good, though. If he hit it just right, he should be able to move the piece up, and away.

But there was no time for any doubts, no time now but to do it.

His two hands locked on the loose metal piece and tightened.

And only now did he look at Tommy, and give him an awkward nod with his helmet.

Gonna be okay, kid. We're gonna get you out of this one.

Sam kept repeating that to himself, repeating, thinking, as if that would make it so.

One. Two.

Gloved hands as tight as possible.

Three.

He pulled up on the bar. At first, he felt nothing but resistance—the other piece was moving. He felt his arm muscles tighten. Sam was in good shape—high school football hadn't been that long ago. But so far, no movement.

He breathed hard, sucking the compressed air in and out, trying to purchase a bit more strength.

He felt his brow furrow, then beads of sweat.

Move, damn it. Let the kid go free. Don't goddamn do this to me when I have only days left.

Move!

And it did, the bar jostled up, startling when it finally shifted. Then after gaining maybe merely an inch it seemed stuck again.

Sam looked down. The jagged end of the bar had cut a longer swath into the kid's suit. Bubbles streamed upward, a crazy line of them escaping to the roof of the room.

Still looking down—no way he could stop now—he kept the levered pressure pulling up.

The bubbles were now mixed with blood.

Another gloved hand fell on his hands wrapped tight around the bar.

Sam turned to the kid, expecting to see the fear, the panic completely in control now, the resignation.

But the eyes looked the same. And the kid did an amazing thing.

He moved his hand under where Sam grabbed the metal, and now—and Sam almost couldn't believe it—the kid pushed upward.

With metal cutting into him, and God knows what the state of his fresh air and exhaust was—and the kid was helping.

People . . .

Amazing goddamn things people can do, Sam thought. *Put them into an incredible situation, and you never know what you're going to see.*

And it helped, the bar now sliding up, now free of the suit, no longer cutting the material, up until . . . a bit more, almost there—

There was nothing holding the kid.

Sam let go of the metal, and wasted no time grabbing Tommy's hand that had just been helping. Fingers wrapped tight.

Sam walked and pulled Tommy behind him. Hell, he'd carry the other diver if he had to. They just had to make it out of the ship, past the hull, and even with his gash, Tommy should be able to partially inflate his suit.

God, we're gonna make it, Sam thought.

Unbelievable.

Step after step, into the corridor, then moving to the

opening. Sam had to take care that they didn't get either of their hoses snagged. Wouldn't want to blow it now. Now when they were so close.

A turn out of the corridor. His light, almost dead, barely caught the outline of the exit.

He turned back to Tommy.

Almost there, partner.

More steps, and Sam was out. He moved away from the jagged opening checking his hoses. Then Tommy was there, still streaming bubbles, still with the dark reddish cloud from his middle.

Sam made a thumbs-up gesture. Time to hit the surface.

Tommy nodded. He'd know enough to take it slow. Just enough air, to get buoyant, a slow controlled ride to the surface.

Sam waited till Tommy started gliding up, all that heavy metal now made to look as though it was filled with air.

And when he couldn't see Tommy anymore, Sam inflated his own suit slowly, until he felt that first bit of lightness, and he started to rise off the floor of San Francisco Bay.

His single thought: *If you have to have a last dive with the Navy, this isn't a bad way to end it.*

And Sam rose up slowly to the surface, and the waiting dive ship.

9

Atlantic City, New Jersey

ANN SAW A MAN STANDING just inside two glass doors.
The glass was flecked with rain, and the man talked on
the phone while great puffs from his cigar spiraled upward, to the high roof of the pier.

"No, wait a minute! The babe is here. Yeah. 'Kay."
This had to be Mr. Nadler. He jammed down the
phone and turned to Ann.

"What took you so long, dollface? I'm a busy man."

"I came right—"

"Yeah, yeah, I know. Lot to see if you haven't been
here before."

"I took a wrong turn."

"Near the games? Designed to get people to stay,
play—" He laughed. "Spend more money."

While Nadler talked, Ann looked around. Above
the doors she saw a painting and the words *The World-
Famous Steel Pier's* . . . and in bigger letters, dripping a
bright blue paint . . . *Diving Bell.*

A small sign hanging over the door read: CLOSED
DUE TO WEATHER.

To the side, barely noticed, a ticket booth.

"So, you're from New York? Broadway, hm? Guess this is a bit unusual for you?"

Ann nodded. "I'm an actress. But—I thought this might be good. Performing with the horses. Something different."

The man took a long drag of his cigar. "Right. Gotcha. We all need work these days, hm? That is why we asked them for someone who could ride, someone with, you know, some ability." Another drag of a cigar. "Doesn't hurt that you're a looker, either."

True enough. You didn't navigate the offices and backstages of entertainment without facing this kind of stuff all the time. Someday, Ann thought, she'd be past it. Past the cheap cigars, the creeps with the bug eyes, and the even creepier ones who let their meaty paws do whatever they wanted to.

She took a breath. Whatever had to be dealt with now . . . she was ready to deal with it.

"Yeah, something different," he continued. "Guess things weren't working out so well back in New York, hm?"

She held his gaze, as she tried to ignore the truth of his words. Another breath. "Things are tough all over."

"Ain't that the truth?" Nadler looked out the glass doors, and the wet spatters hitting the glass, running down to the boardwalk. "But here's the thing . . ."

He took a step closer to Ann, and she felt that sinking feeling.

Don't tell me that the job is gone, that I spent what little money I had to come here, and now there's no job.

She knew her eyes had to be betraying her fears. She never was any good at hiding much of anything. What was that her grandfather used to say on his farm upstate? *Feelings weren't meant for hiding.*

"Something's wrong?" Ann said.

"Not exactly wrong, Ann—it is Ann, right?"

She nodded.

"But we had one of our girls . . . thought she might be pregnant. Didn't want to take any chances. But now it turns out." Another puff, a satisfied smile. "Turns out she isn't!"

Ann had to wonder if Nadler had some kind of connection to the girl beyond being her boss. That would certainly explain the relieved smile.

Ann blew at a few stray strands of her blond hair that seemed to have a mind of their own.

"So there's no job?"

She looked away, the impact of her words now so powerful she thought she could easily start crying. But then thinking: *No way I'm crying, not in front of this creep, no way I'll let him—*

But while she looked away, Nadler reached over and touched her shoulder. "Hey, did I say that? The girl who we thought had to leave doesn't. That's all. The Steel Pier is a big place. I mean, you saw how big; lots of shows, lots of opportunities."

She turned to look at him, her eyes steely locked against those tears. But not wanting to believe too soon that this was all going to turn out okay. "So you do have something for me?"

And in that moment she became aware again of where they stood . . . beside those glass doors, the big picture of the diving bell above her, the ticket booth.

"I'm going to work *here?*"

And the man smiled.

Nadler put an arm on her shoulder and pointed beyond the glass doors. But the arm didn't feel grabby, not at all as if it was the first step in making some kind of play. No, he seemed proud to be showing her what lay outside the doors.

"See that?"

Ann looked out the doors and saw a giant cylindrical chamber.

"That is the world's only diving bell for entertainment purposes."

"What does it do?"

"People go inside, sit down on the metal bench inside, and the hatch is sealed. Then the bell begins an amazing journey down, below the boardwalk, into the sea, down deep, to thirty feet until it rests only a few feet above the bottom."

"And it's safe?"

"Perfectly. Air is pumped in, and the person running the bell talks about the force of pressure, and other amazing facts about the great ocean."

Ann noted portholes ringing the diving bell. "And what do people see?"

Nadler laughed. "Not much. The water is so murky from the surf, the tides, all you can see is a foot or so, flecks of sand, whatever. No big fish sightings I'm afraid. Still"—he squeezed her shoulder—"it's an adventure, something people can do nowhere else."

She turned to Nadler. "So my job is . . . ?"

"You will be the person running the diving bell, Ann. We need someone who's young, attractive—like you. Someone who can reassure the grandmas and the little tykes, let them know it's safe as you shut the door and seal them in. You're perfect."

"Not really a performance job . . ."

Nadler's eyes widened. "What do you mean—not a performance job? Not only will you be reassuring the crowds, getting everyone in, seated, ready—what you do is all *about* performance, Ann. You'll be part of the show from the very beginning. And not only that—see that microphone over there?"

Nadler pointed to a small wooden platform that jutted out of the wall with a microphone on a stand.

"When the people are down there, you'll talk to them."

"About . . . ?"

"You know you're funny? You got a great sense of humor. You talk about the ocean, about going under water, about the adventure."

"I just make stuff up?"

"Nah, we got a whole script for you. All about the temperature, the depth, the pressure—all the stuff I mentioned before. So how about it? As I said, I think you'll be perfect."

And Ann had to think . . . what other choices did she have?

None. And she knew nothing currently waited for her back in New York. She could do this awhile, and maybe something with the diving horses would open up. Save a little money, enough so she could try Broadway again.

Because if there was one other thing her grandfather taught her . . . you just don't give up.

"So how about it Ann? Pay's good. You can start tomorrow. One of the girls in the stage revue even has a spare bed. You'll be all set."

"Okay. I'll take the job," she said quickly, realizing that in truth it wouldn't be hard for Jerry Nadler to find scores of girls who would jump at the chance.

On some level, and not as a letch, she realized he liked her.

"Great. Only one thing we gotta do then, hm?"

Ann's eyes narrowed. Nadler liked holding his cards close, and she felt he had one last secret for her.

"And that is?"

"Babe, you gotta go down."

She pointed out the doors. "In that?"

"Sure. I mean, how are you going to give people the feel of what they're experiencing without doing it yourself? And if someone should get worried—there's a two-way phone in the bell—you have to be the voice reassuring them. And you can reassure them a hell of a lot better if you've been down there yourself."

She looked at the bell sitting there, as sheets of rain pelted the sea green surface.

"And the thing is . . . if you're going to take the job, if you're going to go down, you might as well do it now."

She turned on him.

"Now? In this storm? Now?"

He nodded. "You start tomorrow . . . so . . . 'fraid . . . so."

10

Baffin Island

DENHAM STOOD UP IN THE landing boat. He checked that his camera was lashed securely under the gunwales and covered with a heavy tarp.

Amazing the places I bring a camera, he thought. He looked at the back of the boat, to the actor, Bill Tyler, bundled in a heavy parka, fur cowl pulled tight so the only sign of a head were the puffy breaths of air escaping from his mouth and shivering teeth.

The things actors will do for a job, Denham thought. Though he always told them what they had to look forward to, describing it fully, they always came and quickly started suffering.

Though to be honest, he did describe this shoot in the best possible terms, playing up the adventure, the excitement.

The small boat rocked as Hayes guided his crew rowing toward the shore. Once the *Venture* had anchored beyond the curve of the bay, and protected now by a natural jetty, the stormy conditions eased, as if giving up a losing battle.

Still there was enough chop in the sea to make a

movie star more than green. He imagined that Tyler would be constantly spewing . . . that is, if he had anything left to spew.

Poor bastard. And now that he was stuck here, what could he do? No cabs or buses off this trip. The only way back to civilization was the *Venture*. And part of Denham liked the idea that he had control over these actors. He needed them—he wished he didn't, but without them there could be no story.

And as much as Carl Denham loved capturing images of the world's wonders, he knew that it didn't mean much without a story. A good story raised the images to a mythic level—the bull elephant became more than just a big mammal; it could be some once great hunter's last chance at redemption. The cougar could be the force that made someone else face and defeat their fear.

Where human and animal met, there could always be a story.

It was just unfortunate that also meant actors.

Or in this case, one seasick, cold, and miserable actor.

"Mr. Denham, you want to put in over there?"

Denham turned around and looked in the direction Hayes pointed. There looked to be a natural stony beach, flat, and leading to a rise with some big rocks, tufts of some plant attempting to grow between the cracks. And off to the right, a long jumble of big rocks that formed part of the natural jetty.

"Looks great, Hayes. Take us over."

Carl smiled. Herb Preston smiled back, pointing to the sky. "It's amazing, Carl, but you even got good light."

The boat rocked, hitting some more of the erratic chop that danced in the bay.

Yes, did it get any better than this?

Denham doubted it.

The men quickly unloaded the boat. They put up a tent to protect the camera and audio gear should the dark clouds return. Some food for the men while they shot. Filters for the camera.

And while they did that, Carl could walk the stony beach looking for the best place to shoot. He spotted his actor, Bill Tyler, sitting on a rock. Least he was on shore, the guy had to be grateful for that. He'd give him a few minutes to settle in before talking over the shots Denham wanted to get.

The orcas might be elusive, but they still had another week or so up here before they'd have to give up.

And what if the orcas didn't materialize?

That would be a problem. But he'd do what he always did.

Improvise. The short history of film was based on people of vision making mistakes, and then using those mistakes to achieve greatness.

Denham had a clear vision of what he wanted to do. To go to places people have never seen, film things people only read about—and use it all to tell a story.

"He looks pretty shaky, Carl."

Preston had walked over, and nodded to where the actor sat. Carl looked back.

"Yeah. But at least he's not on the boat anymore. He's gotta be happy about that."

"Want me to talk to him, see how he is?"

Denham shook his head. "No. We start listening to his complaints, and that's all he'll do. Let him get some air, settle down."

Herb had the camera set up, and was checking the lens.

"Herb, I think up here will be a good spot for some shots, you know when the explorer starts thinking about leaving the camp?"

Herb looked at the rolling curve of rocks and boulders that led up and around the cove, out of sight.

"Could be. Want me to take a look and see what it's like up there?"

"Great. Yes. Do a little exploring of your own. I'll go see how things are in the tent and then maybe talk to . . . 'the star.' "

Denham clapped Herb on the back, and then he and Preston walked back to the beach.

"Okay," Denham said to the crew who had carefully arranged the equipment. "Guess we're all set here."

Most of the boat crew sat with Hayes over by the shore, squatting on a scattering of rocks, talking, smoking. They had no interest in the filming process, and that was just fine. Just as long as they stayed away.

He walked over to the actor.

"Hey, Bill, we're just about set here."

Tyler looked up, his poached-egg eyes sunken and masked behind dark circles.

Good thing we're not shooting a musical comedy. As it is, Tyler looked perfect for his part, the haunted explorer.

Denham gestured toward the tent. "Want a bit to eat? I know you—"

Tyler quickly shot up his hand, and Denham thought he might start gagging.

"Didn't think so. All right, soon as Herb comes back, we're going to get some shots of you exploring this area, get some sounds of the black-backed gulls, the water, then shoot you moving inland . . . the beginning of your trek. All right?"

Tyler nodded unenthusiastically.

"Good. So, I think—"

"Carl! Carl!"

Herb's voice rang out over the cove, sounding both scared and excited.

The director turned and looked to the incline of boulders and rocks.

"What is it?" Denham yelled back.

The crew had stood up. Hayes had his rifle by his side. Never went anywhere without it, as if he was ready to hit the trenches of France again.

Some guys never left the war.

"Get up here," Preston yelled.

Then: "You're not going to believe it!"

Denham, followed by Preston and the crew, raced to where Herb stood, waving at them.

And Denham had to wonder: *You can plan, you can organize, but there's always luck. Could it be that luck is about to rear its head?*

For a moment he almost went back to grab the camera.

But in a quick decision, he kept running, thinking, hoping . . . that whatever Herb found looked to be there for a while, ready for them to capture on film.

11

DiGiacomo undid the bolts holding Tommy Hautala's helmet, while another sailor freed Sam. The two helmets came off at exactly the same time.

And the kid was grinning, a big stupid smile plastered on his face.

Is that because the kid doesn't know that he almost died?

But then:

"Thanks, Lieutenant. I was in a bit of trouble down there."

The other sailor offered Sam a cigarette, but Sam waved it away. He had noticed that he breathed harder when he went down after smoking. The ads might say that a smoke was good for your breathing, even with doctors in their ads . . .

But Sam guessed otherwise.

"A bit of trouble?" Sam rolled his eyes at DiGiacomo. "Kid, you were *this close* to becoming a permanent attraction of that wreck."

"Or gettin' the bends. You're one lucky diver," DiGiacomo added.

The two divers started removing the rest of their

suits. The morning sun was bright, and the fear from below faded. Funny how that didn't last. As soon as the event was over, the feeling, the terror, began to fade.

You started to think . . . it was okay. Nothing really bad could have happened.

But then as Tommy stepped out of his suit, the gash through his Navy T-shirt had turned deep crimson, still bleeding.

"God, kid, that's a nasty cut. Get to the infirmary." Sam turned to one of the other sailors. "Get him to the infirmary, okay? Get that looked at."

The sailor walked over to Tommy. "Come on, Hautala. Let's go."

But the young diver got up and came over to Sam.

"Lieutenant, I just want to say thanks again. What you did down there, I mean . . . I know that could have been it."

So the kid wasn't completely oblivious.

"Just part of the job, kid. Now get going."

Tommy smiled, and stepped into the small launch that would speed him over to the Navy docks.

"You want to head back, Sam?" DiGiacomo asked.

But Sam shook his head. The sun glinted on the harbor, the air had turned warm, and he couldn't think of anything better than sitting right where he was.

12

NADLER TOOK THE SMALL SIGN from Ann's hands.

"Look, it's not really dangerous. This sign, 'CLOSED DUE TO WEATHER,' is just because it gets rocky in seas like this, a bit bumpy. But nothing can go wrong. The bell slides down its steel shaft then back up again. We'll have you heading over to your new apartment and new friends in no time."

The only thing Ann felt like she wanted to do now was turn around and walk away. This was like some crazy joke, getting her out here to the diving bell and sending her thirty feet under a roaring sea, all by herself.

"I don't know."

"Look, I don't have all day. Gotta lot to do. Always a headache when we have to close the pier early. But we can do this now, and tomorrow the job is yours. Whaddya say?"

"Straight down and up again?"

"You got it. Just so you know what the whole deal is."

Her eyes were locked on the bell itself, an enemy waiting for her, lurking outside in the rain.

"All right. You'll operate it?"

"Sure, and when you come out, I'll show you the ropes. A kid can do it. Hell, you're almost a kid anyway."

"Do I need any special outfit, or—"

Nadler laughed.

"Nah. We'll just run out there to the bell, get you settled, seal you in. Ready?"

"Yes."

Nadler grabbed the door, and the wind sent drops of rain into the building. He ran out and grabbed a giant lever, and the diving bell opened. He gestured to her to hurry.

Ann ran to the door, bending down a little bit to get in. She saw a metal bench that circled the interior, so people could lean close to the portholes for their personal view of . . . nothing.

"Okay," Nadler said above the wind, "take a seat; you hold the railing in front of you. I'll talk to you from inside the pier. Shutting the door now, okay?"

Ann nodded.

Crazy, she thought. She never liked the ocean, even on a bright sunny day. The few times her mom actually took her (that is, whenever some fella her mother was with decided to go), Ann used to sit on the sand, her back to the crashing waves. The waves, the sea seemed hungry to her, violent.

And it still seemed that way.

"Okay. Have a good dive!"

Nadler slammed the door, and Ann heard the sound of metal hitting metal, followed by the loud locking sounds as he pushed down the outside latch. There now was no way for Ann to get out. She looked up, and saw a small phone—the two-way—with a small sign that read FOR EMERGENCY USE ONLY. ENJOY YOUR TRIP UNDER THE ATLANTIC OCEAN!

She wanted to grab it right now and holler, *Get me the hell out of here!* The dry air smelled so stuffy, a mix of salt and sweat.

Then she heard a voice from the small speaker on the ceiling of the bell.

"Okay, Ann. We're all set here. Here's where you tell the patrons all about holding on to the rail, and how deep they will be going, and to keep their eyes peeled for any creatures of the deep . . . if that was ever likely. Here we go!"

She felt it move. The diving bell started sliding on its massive shaft through a circular opening in the boardwalk. Through the porthole, she watched the boardwalk floor rise above her, then she saw the flooring and pipes, also rising—the hidden underbelly of the boardwalk.

Then underneath the great timbers, a dense jumble of massive poles streaming down from the pier, into the sea. She leaned a bit closer to see the water below.

The gray-green sea rocked back and forth, waves cutting across each other, jockeying for position as if eager to somehow find a way into the diving bell. Then, amazingly the bell slipped slowly below the sea.

And even more amazingly, it became calm. The water took on a greenish color that nearly matched the paint on the bell. Or did for a few feet, before turning a murky gray.

Ann felt the movement of the bell as it made its way down a pole buried in the seafloor.

"Pretty nifty, heh kid?"

Ann plastered her face against the porthole. *Does anyone ever see any fish down here, or anything?* As Nadler mentioned, she could see only a few feet beyond the glass, though she noticed that there was some kind of light from above.

"Here's where you'll start your spiel, Ann. All about the Atlantic Ocean, how many miles deep that ocean gets. Water temperature, and oh yeah the pressure. We have it all written out for you, and—shit!"

He stopped.

The bell came to a halt.

Had she reached the bottom? There was only the glow from whatever light sat on top of the bell, pointing down.

But then she felt something else. The bell rocked.

"Hey, Ann—nothing to worry about. But the bell got hooked up on something. Just give me a minute here."

So she wasn't all the way down. She looked at the two-way phone again. She should reach for that, ask what was wrong, maybe tell Nadler that she wanted to come up now?

And blow the job.

She chewed her lower lip. A habit she tried to lose. Whenever things happened that made her worry, anything that made her anxious—auditioning for a role, or wondering how she was going to pay rent—for some reason her teeth immediately went to her lower lip.

This was funny. For someone who hated the ocean.

To be underwater, stuck.

Funny.

No. Not funny at all. Scary. The black two-way phone sat there. Useless.

The bell wobbled a bit more, then it seemed to lurch down, dropping.

Fast, maybe too fast. *They closed the bell in bad weather for a reason, remember?* Maybe the pole shook, making the bell dangerous in water like this.

It stopped sharply—abruptly enough that her chin bumped against the metal lip of the porthole.

"Okay. All set now. Sorry about that, Ann. It must get a little tricky when the waves kick up. Seemed to get stuck. But everything's okay now. Just got to bring you up."

Ann felt a vibration. The metal container seemed to shake as the force of the current and the waves jostled it.

How deep was I? Ann thought. *Thirty feet? How deep is thirty feet, how far to the surface, if I got out of here?*

Of course, that thought meant nothing since there was no door handle on the inside, no way for her to open that door, and—

What? Let the ocean flood in?

Good idea.

Right, a real good idea. But she had to imagine that panic could make her do just that.

"Ann, gonna bring her up now, okay. Little faster than normal since I guess it's really bad down there, okay?"

Does he want me to answer that? Grab that damn two-way phone and scream like I've never screamed before—and would probably never scream again—get me the . . . hell up!

The bell started up, and that only made the vibration worse, the bell now almost rocking on its pole as it slid up.

God, please make it go fast, please don't let it get stuck—

She closed her eyes. She couldn't bear to watch the water slowly change color, too slowly, going from a sick gray, to a deep green, until finally it became pale.

She opened her eyes. And she saw light, air, the timbers of the boardwalk.

Keep going, keep going, keep—

The rain had turned heavier, now a downpour, hammering the bell, making the outside a blur.

But the diving bell continued to rise up.

Until it finally stopped.

The door popped open. Nadler bent over, peering inside.

"Come on, kiddo, I'm getting drenched here!"

Ann lowered her head, and ran out.

And as she did, entering through the twin glass doors, she heard Nadler. . . .

"Bit rough down there, but least you know what it's like. And hey, congratulations—you're the newest employee of the world-famous Steel Pier!"

And despite everything, Ann had to smile. She had a job and for now that's all that mattered.

13

San Francisco Bay

SAM KELLY HOPPED OFF THE training ship—the converted trawler—and ran to the front to grab the rope thrown by DiGiacomo.

"You don't have to do that, Sam; I got kids who need to learn how to tie a knot."

Sam grinned as he lashed the front of the trawler to one mooring post, then ran aft to get the other rope being tossed by DiGiacomo. He pulled it hard and then gave it a quick double knot.

"How about a beer?" DiGiacomo asked.

"Love one, but I think I better write up a report on the kid and not make him sound like too much of a—"

Someone tapped his shoulder.

"Lieutenant, CO wants to see you."

"Now?" Sam looked at DiGiacomo. "Word must travel fast. CO wants a powwow."

DiGiacomo nodded. Though DiGiacomo outranked Sam, they acted as if they were peers.

But now . . . now—

Sam saw DiGiacomo lower his head as he checked

the ropes and signaled the ensign piloting the boat to cut the engine.

He knows something, Sam thought.

But what?

"I guess . . ." Sam started . . . "I better check with the CO, hm?"

"Yeah, Sam. See you later."

"Right," Sam said.

So Sam started off toward the administration building, near the entrance to the harbor facility.

"Go right in," the CO's secretary said.

Sam smiled, and opened the door with beveled glass, and the gold-lettered name, CAPTAIN ELLIOT BYRNE, USN.

"Afternoon, Captain."

Byrne looked up from his desk.

"Goddamn it, Kelly. God . . . damn it."

Byrne stood up.

"Sir, if it's about the problem with Hautala, I can tell you that we—"

"What? What the hell you talking about, Lieutenant?"

Sam did a quick step backward. So this was not about the kid's almost-fatality in the wreck. "Nothing, sir—I just thought. . ."

" 'Kay. Well, there's nothing else but to give you this."

Byrne held out some papers.

Sam took a quick glance, and immediately knew what they were.

"Discharge orders?"

"Yeah, I know you had a few more days, but guess what? Now you don't. And nor for that matter does anyone else here. The whole Navy dive operation here is to be shut down now, today. That's it."

"And all the divers?"

"Everyone's getting the same papers you have. Cost-cutting. Guess they don't need a West Coast dive operation. At least not this one, here. Cutting expenses throughout the whole damn armed forces. It's a damn bloodbath. Guess with the Great War under our belt, might as well as shit-can the whole thing, hm? Christ."

Sam held the papers. He had been only days away from being out anway. But now, like this, so abrupt—it felt wrong. And not only that, he thought of everyone else who worked the training facility.

"The new men?"

"Early discharge. They'll get about a month's pay. That's about it. God knows where I'll end up."

Sam looked out the window. It was one of those rare perfect San Francisco afternoons, the sun brilliant, the air dry, the sky deep blue, the water calm.

So it was over?

Just like that, his life in the Navy over. Diving, for now, over.

One thing for sure, Sam knew when he'd need another job.

"Should I pack up today?"

Byrne looked up. "Today, tomorrow. Whenever the hell you're ready. This place will become like a ghost town. Me, I'll be gone by midday tomorrow. I can't stand to watch this much stupidity."

Was it stupid? Sam knew that there was a big movement to cut the armed forces down, whittle it down to something small. "America First," the slogan went. No more European wars. Everyone hoped for no more wars at all.

"I'm with you, sir."

Byrne walked around his desk to Sam.

"You've been a great trainer here, Sam; got some great divers, thanks to you. I don't know what the hell you're going to do now . . . what any of us will do. But I can guess one thing. It *will* be important."

Sam extended a hand to the captain.

"Thanks, sir."

"Yeah, and can the 'sir.' You're practically a civilian, Kelly."

Sam smiled. Funny when the military decorum of rank, of orders, slipped away. Like it was some kind of game, let's pretend.

"Guess I better look for a job," Sam remarked. "Got to be some boat somewhere that needs a diver."

Byrne stared at Sam.

"Yeah. Sure. There's gotta be."

Then Byrne walked back to his desk. He sat down, and started shuffling some papers, but not before a quick glance up, and—

"Good luck, Sam."

Sam nodded, and with his discharge papers still in his hands, as if in disbelief, he walked out of the office.

And that evening—

Off the base.

It wasn't a hard decision, now when the facility looked as though it couldn't close fast enough, as if everyone was deserting the sinking ship.

People would come and mothball the boats, and the diving gear. Like Byrne said earlier, God knows where they'd all end up.

Sam did stop by DiGiacomo and the trawler to say good-bye.

Sam had trouble keeping the disappointment out of his voice. DiGiacomo could have told him, could have given him a heads-up.

So damn military . . . keeping the secret.

"Hey, Jock—going to miss diving with you."

"Yeah, me too, Sam."

DiGiacomo was curling the yards of hose; probably getting everything ready for whoever was going to come and do an accounting for the U.S. government. He looked up. "But you were out anyway, right?"

"Yeah. I was gone."

"You got plans?"

"Sure. Lot of plans."

DiGiacomo smiled. "Maybe we can have a beer someday. I mean, if you stick around the Bay Area."

Sam grinned back, letting the old gob off the hook. "Sounds good to me."

An awkward pause from both of them, and then Sam gave a final wave. "See you."

And then walking to the bus stop outside felt like the scariest thing he ever did. Joining the line of other sailors, some smoking and complaining, others quiet in a strange way, all waiting for the green and yellow bus that would take them into the city, take them to whatever would come next.

He had to think . . .

Do we all wonder what's next? Every single one of us?

The future . . .

Damned interesting thing. Interesting, scary, and about the most unknowable thing in the world.

Sam eyed one of the men tapping a Camel out for a pal. *Wouldn't mind one of those,* Sam thought, *now that my diving is done and who gives a damn about my lungs.*

He watched the other sailor, a boy of a sailor, light up the smoke, backlit by the setting sun, the orange at the horizon, the blue sky now deepening to a dark blue, a violet.

Sam made a joke to himself. Made a smile appear on his face.

Stupid little joke.

I know what's next. Sure I do. . . .

The future. My future.

Coming right the hell up.

14

Baffin Island

CARL DENHAM SCRAMBLED OVER THE rocks, clawing at the jagged chunks, trying not to lodge his leg in the maze of small cracks and crevasses.

But as he neared Herb he heard something, a sound somehow shielded from the beach by this rise and the wind.

The low rumble of animal noises—so many of them, a steady roar.

Denham hurried his climb . . . until he reached a high point, only yards away from a grinning Herb.

"Holy . . . mackerel," Denham said. "Unbelievable!"

Herb's smile went from ear to ear. "Nobody's ever seen anything like this Carl. Nobody!"

Denham just wanted to look, to soak in the sight, while he tried to figure out what it was.

On the other side of the rise, around the curve of the bay, sat an army of sea lions, some waddling, some rising up on rocks, all of them making noises.

"Something, hm, Carl?"

"Oh, Herb . . . you did good. We have to get this."

"Should I get Tyler, get him in the shot?"

Carl waved it off. "Nah, we get these babies on film, we can cut him in later. I just want to get this down on film. How many are there, God . . . ?"

Preston appeared next to Carl. "Got to be . . . I don't know—a couple hundred? Maybe more."

"They're like a herd. Wonder why they came here?" Herb turned back.

"Maybe no Inuits come here? You see the smoke? It's all gone. They've moved on. Could be it's safe. You see over there?"

Herb pointed to the back of the sea of seals. At first Denham didn't see anything more than more lumbering, shaking seal bodies jostling for position.

Then he saw them.

"Babies."

"Right. They must come here, give birth, some kind of seal ritual."

Denham clapped Herb's shoulder. "You know, for finding this you deserve a raise."

"Really?"

"That is, if I had any money for a raise. But our day will come, Herb . . . our day will come . . ."

Denham walked with Herb and Preston. In a few minutes, the light had changed, the storm clouds now completely melted away, and now he could look up and see giant blots of blue dotting the white cloud cover.

"How do you think the light is?" Denham said.

Herb looked up at the sky, then the sea.

"Not bad. But—love to shoot them from the other angle."

"You mean from behind the herd?" Denham could see that the seals went flush to the jagged wall . . . as if they knew the stone wall gave their pups protection.

"I dunno, Herb. How the hell you going to do that? Let me get some shots here, at least."

Denham took the camera, and then looked through the viewfinder, first scanning the scene, before starting to turn the crank. Then he began a slow pan.

Though Herb was his operator, Denham only felt like a real filmmaker when he turned the crank himself.

"Beautiful. What a shot. Going to look amazing on the big screen."

"Carl—"

"What Herb?" Denham said without pausing. "Want to do some of this yourself?"

"I see a way to do it. It can be done."

"What's that?" Denham kept on cranking until he had the camera turned nearly one hundred eighty degrees, looking out at the sea, now dappled with glistening foamy spits that caught the sunlight. "Just gorgeous."

Then Denham stopped and glanced up.

"If I go over there, I could get to that cliff, see where it curves in a bit," Herb remarked.

"Yeah. But—"

"I think it curves in just enough so that I can get a shot. Light in the back. Looking out at the whole field, the pups in front. Be a great shot, Carl."

Carl studied the area pointed out by Herb. "You know what—you're right. Come on, let's go—"

Herb grabbed his arm. "Hey, Carl. There's not room for both of us. Going to be tricky going around the herd, getting in here with just me and a camera."

Carl looked Herb in the eyes. They had had similar discussions before. When there was a shot for one person to get. Denham was the director, Herb the camera operator. Herb was good; he deserved to get this shot. And it could make the film.

Preston, standing a little behind, cleared his throat. "Isn't it a little dangerous? All those sea lions . . ."

Carl turned to him. Preston liked to fret. Always the Ivy League worrier, seeing problems everywhere. Sometimes Denham wondered why he kept the kid around.

"Sea lions, seals, whatever, they look like they're pretty calm to me. We're not hunting them. Just shooting a movie."

"Okay. Just that there's so many of them."

Herb tapped Denham's arm. "Carl, if I'm to try for the shot, I better go now. Every minute we lose more light."

"Yeah, go on. We'll watch from here."

And he watched Herb pick up the camera, and start cutting, moving away from the sea lions, then around to the cliff, to the curved section . . . and the shot of a lifetime.

15

Baffin Island

DENHAM WATCHED HERB MOVE ACROSS the rocks. At one point, the cameraman had to cut across a line of brownish-gray sea lions. And though a few raised their snouts and roared at his intrusion, they didn't move.

"Fat lazy things, hm?" Denham said.

"What are they here for?" Preston said. "Some kind of seal vacation?"

Preston laughed at his joke.

"What the *hell* is he doing?"

Denham turned to see Hayes standing next to him, rifle in hand.

"Herb? Getting me the shot of a lifetime."

Hayes scanned the sea of animals that filled the rocky inlet. "Where did you send him?"

"I didn't send him anywhere, Hayes. See over there? There's some kind of natural cove there, right where that rock wall begins. He's going to sneak in, set the camera up, and get a shot looking out over the sea."

"That's stupid."

"What do you mean . . . that's stupid?"

Denham looked back to see that Herb was only minutes away, but something in Hayes's voice made him alarmed.

"Wh-what do you mean?" Denham repeated.

Preston, standing beside Denham, shifted uneasily on his feet.

"Look over there, in the back. All those damn pups." Hayes was pointing.

"Right, they'll be in the foreground of the shot—"

"No. Don't you see how they're set up? They got the bulls in the outer ring, nasty big guys, watching out, protecting—and there! The females, with the pups to the back."

Now Hayes tapped Denham's shoulder.

"It's all about protection, Denham . . . protecting the babies. And you sent him over there?"

"I told you, I didn't send—"

Denham spun around. In a matter of moments, what had been merely the adventure of getting a breathtaking shot turned suddenly nightmarish. And Denham didn't like fear. No, he was fine as long as everything was under control. But once things turned dangerous—his mouth went dry, his heart raced.

He yelled to the camera operator.

"Herb! Herb—come back!"

Denham waved, then joined by Preston and Hayes, all three now waving, yelling.

But whether it was the wind or that his goal was close, Herb didn't acknowledge them and kept going.

Right to the indentation, just behind the collection of pups.

They screamed some more, waving frantically.

"I'll go get him," Denham said.

But Hayes grabbed Denham's arm.

"No. If he sees us, maybe, just maybe, he can slip away. But you or I head over there, it could get the entire rookery crazed. Guess you never seen one of those bastards attack, never seen them fight each other?"

"They're seals. What do you mean fight?"

"Yeah, leopard seals. When two males go at each other, or even when they face off against a polar bear . . . that snout makes any wolf snout look like a toy. And all that weight, lunging, snapping—"

Denham broke away from Hayes and yelled again. But now Herb was at the indentation, quickly setting up the camera, turning to face in their direction.

He stopped. He saw them waving; he waved back.

"Fool," Hayes said. "He doesn't know we're waving at him to get himself back here."

They kept on motioning, but all Denham could see was Herb leaning down, hand on the crank, and—

The wind shifted.

He heard a sound, a low, rumbling roar . . . like an engine, but then steadily building in volume.

The male bulls, raising their heads in anger.

"Christ, Denham," Hayes said.

"Carl," Preston said, "what are we—"

Herb cranked the camera, oblivious of what was happening. Some of the pups scurried away, guided, herded by females. The sound grew loud enough that Denham finally saw Herb look up. Look up, and see movement, that sea of animals shifting positions.

"Forget the goddamn camera," Denham muttered. Something he'd never thought he'd say. "Forget it. Move. Move Herb . . ."

There was no need for them to yell or wave anymore. Herb could finally see what was happening. The seals were moving, shifting, and in a matter of moments, the pups were all away and the bulls had tightened around Herb, trapping him.

Just that fast, Herb was surrounded. The horrible growling of the dozens of creatures swelled, building to *something*.

Some kind of primal group signal that would trigger what would happen next.

16

Atlantic City, New Jersey

ANN KNOCKED ON THE DOOR of the third-floor walk-up apartment, 3B. The stairwell had been filled with the sounds of radios, people talking, and the smell of countless meals, trapped in the airless space.

She still felt rattled by her trip in the diving bell. Sure, nothing had happened, but the terrible fear she felt, the panic—it still made her stomach tighten just to think about it.

But that was the one and only time she would have to do that. In a way, she was glad that she didn't get the job working with the diving horses. What would that be like, jumping off a platform, flying into the ocean while an audience watched?

That sounded even more terrifying.

She knocked again.

No answer.

Maybe her new roommates were out. She knocked a third time, and now she heard footsteps on the other side, and the door opened.

"Yeah?"

The girl was young, but her bleary eyes spoke of either tiredness or maybe a slug of one gin too many. The girl's brunette hair was up in curlers, and dabs of cream dotted her cheeks.

Yeah. . . . as if she didn't expect me at all, thought Ann.

"Hi, I'm the new—er, I just came to the Steel Pier, to—"

"Oh, right." The girl didn't smile, but she did open the door wider. "Yeah, Nadler said you were coming."

The girl held the door open with about as little enthusiasm as she could muster. As Ann walked in, she smelled the stale odor of cigarette smoke. She had hoped that they wouldn't be smokers—such a horrible smell.

After Ann was inside, the girl shut the door.

"I'm Ellie. Susan isn't here; she's out with her guy. Might not be back tonight, if you know what I mean. Your bed is in her room." Ellie looked right at Ann. "Could be a problem sometimes, if you know what I mean."

Ann nodded, guessing she did "know what she meant."

"Come on. I'll show you."

Though the girl had to be in her early twenties, she walked slowly, shuffling down the hallway.

Must have been a rough night.

"That there is the kitchen." A look back at Ann. "But I guess you can see that. And over here, the bathroom. Gets kinda jammed in the morning."

A few more steps, and Ellie turned and pushed open a door.

The room, painted a pea soup green, was a mess. "She kinda dresses and runs, you know?"

Clothes were strewn on the floor, a dress, some lingerie, a pair of high-heeled dance shoes. "Susan's a bit of a party girl, a real flapper. Doesn't know that those days are over. But between the pier and her beaus, she does all right." Ellie dug into the pocket of her chinoise robe and pulled out a pack of Lucky Strikes. She tapped one out, and plucked it into her mouth.

She offered one to Ann, who politely held up a hand.

"Not a smoker? Too bad. This place gets like a firetrap sometimes." Ellie pulled out a lighter and with one hand deftly lit the smoke. "Susan's fun though— if you don't mind the mess. She really cares about people."

"I—I don't mind the mess."

Ellie laughed. "So you *do* think it's messy?"

"No, I meant—"

Ellie reached out and touched Ann's arm. "Hey, honey, it's okay. It's messy, the place is smoky, sometimes we have a belt or three too many. It's okay. You'll be fine."

Ann smiled, and realized that—despite everything—she was starting to relax, and starting to like this girl with her weary attitude and funny sense of humor.

"So, that's your bed there. Susan's stuff is on it, but

you can just move that junk. She won't be back tonight." Another touch to Ann's arm. "You can trust me on that one."

Ann put down her small brown suitcase.

"That all you got?"

"I have more back in New York City, at a friend's apartment. I just brought this to see what I need."

"Well, you can take a drawer, I guess. Move her stuff. Then, hey come on into the kitchen and have a drink. If we're going to be roomies, toots, we better start swapping hard-luck stories, hm?"

Ann walked into he kitchen and saw Ellie with another cigarette, a foot up on one chair, and the bottle of Gordon's Gin on the table.

"Pour you a glass?"

Ann didn't drink, not really. A bit of wine maybe. She couldn't remember when she last tasted hard liquor.

But she said, "Yes."

Ellie filled the slim glass a third of the way.

"So—" Ellie picked up her glass. "Here's mud in your eye, sis."

And Ann grabbed her glass and took a deep sip of the icy, clear liquor. Like liquid fire, it burned her tongue, then sent a burning feeling shooting down her throat. Bitter, yet the glow when it hit her stomach felt good.

"There you go. So what show you working?"

"What?" Ann said.

"You doing the revue? You a dancer, or—"

"I do dance. But I'm an actress—a comedienne, really."

Ellie smiled, almost a smirk. "Really? Didn't know the pier needed actresses."

"They don't. But I got hired to dive."

Ellie stubbed out the cigarette, and Ann was glad to see that she didn't tap out another.

"Oh, you mean the horses."

"Yes, I—"

"Never catch me doing that. Jumping off that high platform on a damn horse. Right into the ocean? Those girls are a little strange . . . know what I mean."

"Yes. I mean, no . . . but that's what I was hired to do—but not what I'm doing."

"No? Working the Ford display? Now, that could get boring."

"No. I was hired to dive, but they don't need me now with the horses, not there. I'll be running the diving bell."

And Ellie burst out laughing.

"The diving bell? Honey, you're going to need a lot of gin to get through *that* job."

"Why? It doesn't seem hard, putting people in, telling them about—"

" 'The mystery of the sea' . . . 'you are now twenty feet below the surface of the great Atlantic Ocean' . . . every day, dozens of times day." She laughed some more and shook her head. Then she took the bottle and poured another splash into Ann's glass.

"Good luck, Annie . . . you're going to need it."

But Ellie's laughing seemed so good-natured that Ann had to laugh too, smile, and then grab her gin glass to take another cautious sip.

17

Baffin Island

CARL DENHAM GRABBED HAYES'S ARM.

"We've got to do something!"

Denham turned and looked back at Herb. The male sea lions had edged closer, the sound now filling the cove. The pups were nowhere to be seen.

"Move, damn it. Get the hell—"

And then as if reading Denham's mind, Herb started to run around the circling group of leopard seals.

"Drop the camera," Denham muttered again. "Drop the goddamn—"

But Herb held it tight.

He wasn't the only one moving. Hayes ran to the right to a jumble of large boulders, chunks of granite that sat at strange angles, jagged edges everywhere. But Hayes didn't pause, running full-out with his rifle, to a high point.

Denham turned back to Herb.

His attempt to escape was cut off.

Denham watched one large bull seal leap forward, and then just like that, Herb was down. Now Denham could see Herb scrambling to get up, while another pair of seals raced forward, onto him.

Denham heard a new sound.

A scream, cutting through the rumbling growls and barks of the seals.

Then finally, cutting through it all.

A shot, then another . . . and another.

Turning to Hayes, on the rocks, the gun at his shoulder.

Shooting one round after another. The distance wasn't bad, and Hayes had a good perch from up there. Still, could the ex-doughboy, medals and ribbons not withstanding, be sure he was hitting the seals and not Herb?

The shots kept coming and, as if finally getting the message, the crowd of seals backed away, maybe scared by the sight of the others dropping dead in their tracks.

They kept backing away, some even scurrying into the water, others just moving far away from the carnage. One of the crew ran up to Hayes carrying what looked like more cartridges.

Hayes wasn't the happiest crewman on the *Venture* . . . but no doubt at times like this, he was the guy you wanted with you.

Denham watched Hayes reload his rifle, but the pack around Herb had cleared. Carl ran over to Hayes. Other crewmen were already racing there, some with more guns.

"We can get to him now," Hayes said. "Come on!"

Denham nodded. In situations like this, it was clearly Hayes who was in charge.

The pack of seals now seemed to be aware that these other mammals walking toward Herb were not to be bothered. Only one or two would raise a snout, make a snarling noise, then turn away.

The universal language of blood, Denham thought. *Every animal knows what it means. The smell, the color—a flag of warning.*

Hayes led the way, still with his gun held close as if he might be entering a French village, leading a squad of black soldiers fighting not only for their country but their future.

Denham well knew the bitterness Hayes carried with him about how that all turned out. The war should have been their gateway to getting everything they wanted in white man's America. This time, this war, it didn't turn out that way. Might have been the Depression, or the times; everyone was sick of the fighting and hoping that war was a thing of the past.

Now they scrambled over a scattering of rocks, tricky to keep one's balance.

Denham forced himself to look ahead. To look at Herb on the ground, expecting the worst.

But Herb was moving his head, as if struggling to sit up.

"God," Hayes said. He turned to some of the crew behind him. "Get the stretcher, some bandages, and move!"

A few crewmen ran back to the beach.

And then they were there, in front of Herb.

Denham did a quick scan of his friend, the camera operator. He had been bitten on one arm, and he also had some bite marks on his torso, oozing blood. Nothing too bad there.

But his right leg . . .

Something had obviously wrapped its maw around it and chomped down, *hard*. Denham could see the white of bone, the swirling mix of red, gushing.

What was left of Herb's lower leg remained attached to the kneecap—but barely.

Denham went to his friend's head and cradled it.

Why isn't he screaming? Why isn't he howling out in pain? Had to be shock. Sometimes the sensation just shuts things down. Thankfully. Denham could only imagine the waves of pain that Herb would feel—if his brain hadn't walled off that area.

"H-how bad is it, Carl? The bite, it felt—"

"Hey, you're gonna be fine, Herb. Just fine."

A quick glance back, and Denham watched Hayes grab a roll of gauze from someone, and quickly whip out a yard.

"This is going to hurt, Herb."

Hayes began wrapping the area just below the knee.

"We gotta stop the bleeding."

"Right," said Herb. "Right. But," he turned back to Denham, "it's going to be okay, right? I'm going to be fine?"

"Sure. It's going to be okay, Herb. You just relax. Hey look, here come the guys with a stretcher." Denham's tone was soothing, as some crewmen, led by Englehorn, scrambled over the rocks and approached.

Englehorn came and squatted beside the camera operator.

"We have a first-aid kit, Carl, Do you want to—"

"No," Hayes said. "You should get him out of here, back to the boat, and . . . do what we can do there."

Right, thought Denham. *Do what we can do . . .*

Because you didn't have to have a medical degree to know that Herb's leg . . . had to be a goner.

"Okay, Herb—they're going to move you onto the stretcher. Get you back to the *Venture*."

The man's eyes were wide, wild with fear, and pain. Herb kept licking his lips. His eyes blinked, the closest thing to a nod that he could manage.

And Denham backed away as six people tried to move Herb as carefully as they could.

Once on the *Venture*, Billy Clarke, the ship's semi-official medic, bandaged Herb's wound as best he could, covering the area with hydrogen peroxide and giving as much morphine to the camera operator as he could stand.

Denham and Englehorn conferred out in the corridor.

"Once that morphine wears off, he's going to be screaming," Denham said.

"Then we'll just shoot him up again." Englehorn nodded, then looked at his friend. "You know the leg is gone. I mean, Clarke is in no position to cut it off. But there's no hope."

"I know."

"I told Hayes to set a course for Halifax, fast as possible. We've radioed ahead. They'll have an ambulance waiting."

"Good."

"Guess this messes up your film."

Denham smiled. "Not the first time. But the important thing is to get Herb some help."

"Glad to hear you say that, Denham."

"Hm?"

"Sometimes . . . I think all you care about is your movie."

"Oh, I do care. But it's people that make pictures, Captain. And Herb has been with me from the beginning."

"With luck, he can still be with you."

"Yeah. Maybe."

Englehorn turned away. "I'd best see to the bridge . . ."

But then he stopped, and turned back to Denham.

"One of the crew ran out and grabbed the camera. Pretty brave, I say. So whatever Herb shot, that whole scene there, you've got the film."

Denham smiled at that. "I'm glad. And you know what, when this is all over, I bet Herb will be glad too."

"Yeah, I imagine he will."

Englehorn continued topside. Denham stood there for a moment, alone, thinking about what was next, what would happen, wondering what the future held. Then he turned back to the small room turned into an infirmary, opened the door, and went back to the bedside of his good friend.

18

San Francisco

SAM KELLY LEAFED THROUGH THE *San Francisco Examiner* classifieds, thinking . . . *Where'd they hide all the jobs?*

He knew things were bad—but Sam had skills, he could actually type, file a report, knew his way around a car engine, and—oh yeah, by the way—he was a trained helmet diver.

The classifieds had nothing.

Good thing he had a little nest egg saved from the Navy. But how long would that last?

He did see a listing for an employment agency and gave the number a call.

A woman with a nasal accent answered the phone.

"Hel-lo?"

More of a question than anything.

"Yeah, I saw your listing and I'm—"

"Anyone looking for employment must come in and fill out an application and pay the fee."

"Fee? You mean I got to pay to find a job?"

"That is how we operate, sir. If you want our assistance in procuring employment, then you will have to—"

Sam hung up.

Time for a different plan. No jobs in the papers, the agencies scamming and skimming from the out-of-work. But he could walk around and see what was available.

So on a beautiful late spring day, he hit the streets of San Francisco.

He walked as though he was in some kind of competition, from the heights of Telegraph Hill, to the area south of Market, then back to the Embarcadero.

To see . . . nothing.

In Golden Gate Park he noticed the rows of boxes that back east they had started calling Hoovervilles, makeshift shelters for the down-and-completely-out.

Something had to happen to save this country.

All one had to do, Sam knew, was look at what was happening in Europe to get an even deeper sense of fear. Enough poverty, enough hunger, and enough desperation—and anything could happen.

This country was too damn good to go that route.

Could be the next election might bring the change needed.

Sam sure the hell hoped so.

He stopped at Woolworth's and asked about a possible job, mumbling about the Navy. But his question there—and anywhere else he tried—brought a smirk, then a look in the manager's eye's that said . . . *poor bastard.*

I'm not panicked yet, Sam thought. But could panic be that far away?

No money, no job, that would be a new experience for a kid from Flatbush who had worked ever since he was twelve, from delivering the *Eagle* to training new divers.

Already his time with the Navy seemed unreal.

Did it happen, was I really a lieutenant in charge of training divers?

He saw a small department store on Fremont—Murray's.

Kelly walked in and walked up to a young woman behind a perfume counter, her eyes expectant.

Sales must be hard to come by. . . .

"Yes, sir, can I help you?"

Sam smiled.

"Could be. I was wondering if the manager was in?"

The glow faded from the woman's face.

"The manager? He's—" The woman turned, and pointed to a small room that overlooked the small department store. "—up there."

"Thanks," Sam said.

He saw a door in the back—no sign on it but it clearly led to the manager's office. He opened it, and quickly trotted up the few flights of stairs.

At the top of the landing, he saw another door, with the words STORE MANAGER on it.

Sam knocked.

"Yes, come in."

Sam opened the door. The man inside, pudgy, not much older than Sam but already with thinning hair and a face permanently scrunched up, looked up.

"Can I help you?" the manager said with a decidedly suspicious look.

"Could be. I just left the service, Navy, worked down at the harbor. So, I'm starting to look for a job as a civilian."

The manger stood up. At his full height, he was at least a foot shorter than Sam. Still that didn't stop him from hurrying over and staring up, right at Sam's face.

"Did someone send you here?"

"No, I just have been hoofing it, looking at places that might need—"

"Need? Did someone tell you we need people?"

"No. I just said—"

"Let me tell you something, sailor. We have been *firing* people. I have half the people I had a year ago. And though they don't know it, even they are in danger of getting canned. So—is this some kind of joke or something?"

Panic. Sam could see it in the manager's eyes.

"Okay. I got it. Sorry."

Sam turned and started out of the office.

"Hey, look. I'm sorry," the small man said. "Things are bad. You served your country. There should be a job, lots of jobs for you guys to pick from. But I got to tell you, you're not going to find anything here."

Sam looked back.

"Here?"

"San Francisco. The city. Maybe any city. You know, you might try getting out to the valley. They sometimes hire seasonal workers for the farm. Not a lot of money. But it's something. Something, you know?"

"Right. Better than nothing?"

"Exactly."

Sam smiled. "Thanks for the tip."

Then he turned and walked out.

Bad days, Sam thought. And for a moment he wished he could be almost anywhere else.

Sam Kelly entered the Turk Street Hotel, a fleabag dump even for the Tenderloin—his home for now.

He walked up to the desk clerk. The guy, with sunken, haunted eyes, looked like a perfect target for his question.

"Say, pal, I was wondering . . ."

The guy looked up, and Sam saw that he was studying a racing form. Probably sank whatever lousy pay he got for this job straight into the ponies. And that didn't seem to be going too well.

"Yeah?"

"Yeah, see I just left the Navy. . . ."

The clerk's eyes narrowed. He probably heard every hard-luck, looking-for-a-job story. Probably constantly had people trying to stretch their room rent, which was already ridiculously low.

"I'm looking for a place to get a drink. Nothing fancy, just a few bats and balls, hm?"

The clerk grinned.

This at least was no problem.

"Sure. Not far from here actually, a joint on Sutter, near the hospital. I'll write the number down, and just tell them Joey sent you."

"You Joey?"

The clerk shook his head.

"No. That's just what you say."

Sam grinned. "Good. I'll remember that. Joey."

"Right. Good booze, good people."

"All I need right now is the booze."

"Right." The clerk handed Sam the piece of paper with the building number. "It's downstairs. Cops know about it. No one really cares anymore."

"I'm sure," Sam said.

He took the slip of paper . . . thought about grabbing a nap in his dingy room.

But right now hitting a speakeasy seemed like about the best idea he had all day.

Sam sat on the stool.

The joint was set up like a normal bar, with rows of bootleg hooch with familiar labels on the wall, tables scattered on the floor. Off to the corner there looked like there was a spot for a band. Could be the place got a bit jazzy on a Saturday night.

Of course, this was a late afternoon, in the middle of the week.

Still, Sam wasn't alone. A few other reprobates sat around at the other end of the bar doing a fine job of kicking down a "ball"—a shot of whiskey—followed by a foamy "bat," a small tumbler of beer.

A couple sat at a table, with all the earmarks of an illicit romantic meeting, sitting close, whispering, Sam catching the occasional kiss.

Been a while since I've been there too, Sam thought.

He had a girl back in Flatbush, but that fell apart when he went into the Navy. Since then . . . a few dates, and one strange encounter last New Year's Eve that he'd sooner forget.

Can be scary waking up the next day and seeing exactly what you spent the night with. . . .

But girls—that was a part of life he wanted to somehow get going too.

A job. A real place to live. A girlfriend.

A life.

Sounded damned difficult, maybe impossible.

"Another?" the bartender asked.

"Sure," Sam answered.

And it wouldn't be long before Prohibition ended, he thought. A great experiment gone wrong. Take something humans have been doing for thousands of years and make it illegal.

Let the crime bosses step in and make a killing.

Every beer, every shot, every bottle of booze making them wealthier and more powerful.

After the election, Sam guessed that would all change. That and hopefully everything else.

The bartender put down the beer and a shot.

Sam reached for his wallet.

"Paid for, pal."

Sam looked up. "What, what do you mean?"

He felt a hand on his shoulder.

"Drinks on me, Lieutenant."

Sam turned around to see the goofily grinning face of Tommy Hautala.

Tommy looked up at the bartender. "And the same for me. I gotta talk to my old teacher here."

Sam laughed and shook his head, as Tommy took the stool next to him.

"So finding you wasn't hard. You mentioned the Turk Street Hotel. And the clerk told me you were looking for a watering hole."

"And a watering hole I found. By the way, you sure you have enough greenbacks to be buying me a drink?"

Tommy grinned. "For the man that saved my life? Absolutely. But I also consider it an investment. In my future. In *our* future."

Sam kicked back the whiskey, enjoying the quick burn.

"*Our* future? Do tell. I thought our future ended when we left the base with nothing but our duffel bags."

Tommy waved a finger at Sam. "See, sir, that's where you're—"

"And you can stop calling me 'sir.' It's just Sam now, okay?"

"Yes, s . . . Sam. But as I said, that's where you're wrong. I have found us a great opportunity."

Sam laughed. "There's that word again. *Us.* Maybe you just better spill the beans and tell me what you're up to, all right?"

The bartender slid down to their end. "Another round?"

Sam waved him away. "We're okay now, thanks." The bartender moved away. "I want to keep my wits while you tell us about 'our' future."

"So as soon as I left the base, I went down to the wharf. And you know the fishing boats, they're all busy but they don't need nobody. But down there, guess what I found?"

Sam took a sip of beer.

"I'm clueless."

"A dive ship, Lieutenant—I mean Sam."

"A dive ship. Salvage and recovery?"

"No. That's the great part. It's not one of those ships trolling for a wreck and whatever garbage they bring up."

"Then what was she?"

Hautala leaned close, scanning the room as if he was about to reveal a secret that could change history.

"She was a . . . *pearl* ship."

Sam took a breath. "A pearl ship? What is she doing here?"

"Had to come to Frisco for some work on her engine. But some of their divers got into trouble. Something with the cops, I think. They're due to set sail."

"So . . . you got a job? Diving for pearls?"

Hautala's grin widened. "No, not just me. The two of us."

"Really?"

The kid wasn't much good at stretching the truth.

Sam smelled something funny and kept his eyes locked on Tommy. The kid sensed the scrutiny, and pushed his shiny blond hair off his forehead.

"Yeah, they could use the two of us."

"That so? That's how it all happened?"

The kid rolled his eyes. "Well. To be honest . . . Sam. No. They asked me about my training, how much deep ocean diving, all that stuff. I was about to lose the job. But then I mentioned you. How we worked together."

"Oh, is that what it was? We worked *together*?"

"Okay. You were my teacher. But they wanted us both. Actually . . . they would only take me with you."

"Pearl diving?"

"Yes."

"Never did that. Not sure—"

"They just need trained deep divers, Sam. They have one other, so there's a team of three, working together. The captain, a Portuguese guy, said, 'It's a no worry . . . train you both . . .' "

"That what he sounded like?"

Tommy laughed.

"Whatcha think, Sam?"

Sam looked at the kid. Not like there were a lot of opportunities on the table. Not a lot at all.

And it was diving—what he knew so well.

"Guess it wouldn't hurt to go talk to the captain."

Tommy slapped Sam's back, then acted as if that had been too much an act of familiarity. Sam grabbed his beer and downed it.

"Tomorrow morning okay?" Sam asked.

"Yeah, they don't sail till the next day, at best."

"Good. Tomorrow then. You can meet me at the hotel."

Tommy looked down at the bar floor. "That's the other thing, um, Sam."

"Yeah?"

"I don't have a place to stay, so I was wondering if I could—"

Now it was Sam's turn to laugh. "Sure. You got it. The floor is yours."

"Great."

Sam stood up. He wasn't ever a heavy drinker, and the bats and balls were taking their toll.

"One question, Tommy."

"Shoot."

"Where is the ship going? Where exactly will these deep dives for pearls take place?"

"That's the best part! It will be sailing to the Indian Ocean, off Sumatra. It's going to be incredible."

"If you say so, kiddo, if you say so. Never been anywhere near that part of the world myself. Or you either, I imagine, hm? Now, let's find someplace where we can get a really cheap meal."

And Sam led the way out of the dingy speakeasy.

19

Atlantic City, New Jersey

ANN SHUT THE DOOR OF the diving bell. She wore a forest green skirt and matching blazer, all provided by the pier. The blazer sported a patch that read "The World-Famous Steel Pier . . ." Then, in bigger letters, "Diving Bell."

She pressed the latch down—like an elevator, the bell wouldn't move unless the latch was completely locked into place. Onlookers behind her watched the process, awaiting their turn for a great adventure under the sea.

She went over to the microphone and picked up the script, just as she had done all morning.

"Ladies and gentleman, the world-famous Steel Pier Diving Bell has been locked and you are about to undertake the underwater adventure of a lifetime. Sit forward, close to the portholes, as we take you under the ocean, to the bottom of the sea . . ."

That is, she thought, *if you could consider a mere thirty feet or so the bottom of the sea.* Still, the people, a collection of young families, seemed more than excited stepping into the bell. It *was* a great adventure for them, and Ann's performance was an important part of it.

"I am now beginning to lower the diving bell down. You will pass below the great timbers that support the Steel Pier, timbers that resist fierce ocean waves and even hurricanes."

A gauge on the wall told her the depth of the bell. And as soon as the portholes began to hit water, she continued . . .

"You are now entering a world unknown to most people, the world of the deep sea. Air compressors on the pier will keep a steady supply of fresh air being pumped into the diving bell."

She took another look at the gauge.

"You will notice that the deeper we go, the less light there is. And as we descend, color also fades as you enter the mysterious world of the ocean. Keep your eyes open for any signs of life. Fish such as flounder and bluefish are often seen."

In truth, Ann guessed all they would see would be the swirl of silt in the churning sea. Had anyone ever seen a fish come up to a porthole?

Another glance at the gauge, and she stopped the bell. Nadler said that even if she did nothing, like an elevator, the bell would come to rest. But she felt more in control stopping it herself.

That, and she felt as if these people's lives were in her hands. For the few minutes they were down there, she controlled their fate.

It was an empowering feeling she had never had before.

"You have now reached the bottom of the sea."

Though again, the bell rested on a bumper a foot above the ocean floor.

"The Atlantic Ocean off this coast can vary in temperature from thirty-five degrees to seventy degrees Fahrenheit, depending on the season. Right now the water temperature outside is sixty-five. The currents that hug the coast of Atlantic City can run all the way up to the state of Maine, and beyond. And don't forget—keep your eyes peeled on the porthole . . . you never know what you may see."

Now Ann looked at a timer, a clock that told her when to bring the diving bell up. This was the fun part, for the riders at least. The bell came up fast, rocketing to the surface—a surprise that sent them out laughing and excited, a good ad for the next batch of aquanauts.

"We are prepared to bring you back to the safety of the surface. So hold on as the diving bell brings you up from the ocean floor."

She hit a button, and the bell raced to the surface now. People on the pier could look down and see the dome of the bell break the surface, shooting out a giant foamy circular wave.

Then the bell came up the rest of the way slowly until the huge cylinder, still with water streaming off it, locked into place, level with the boardwalk.

She walked over and unlocked the door, something that could be done only from the outside.

"Have a good trip?" she said, as she was instructed to do for each group.

And out they streamed, talking among themselves, still giddy from rocketing to the surface. Ann waited until the bell was empty, then went over and undid the chain holding back the next group of underwater explorers.

She took their tickets, and they streamed in.

And as they did, Ann looked up at a big clock hanging in the hall of the pier. Three more hours until she was done for the day.

Her first day, and already she was watching the clock.

But it was better than being hungry.

Better than being on the street.

And she told herself: *It's only temporary. Something else will happen, something else will come up.*

It had to. . . .

Ann entered the apartment and saw Ellie, in the kitchen, feet stretched out on a chair.

"Hi, Annie—how was your first day?"

Ann smiled. "It was okay. Nothing went wrong at least, the people were nice . . ."

"And? That's all?"

"It's a little boring. Don't know how I can do it six days a week, all day. I'll probably go mad."

"Welcome to the club. Here, have a little hooch. Keeps the madness away."

Ellie took a glass and poured some of the clear liquor.

"Maybe I better eat something first. I barely had anything to—"

"Drink. Come on, I don't like to drink alone. And with Susan still . . . away, you're my new pal."

Ann smiled and sat down on a kitchen chair.

"Feels good just to sit down."

"Yes, kiddo—that's for sure. So, guys make any passes?"

"No, now that you mention it." Ann laughed. "Maybe it's this outfit. I look like I should be working the lobby at that new Radio City Music Hall when it opens. Did you hear about what the usherettes will be wearing?"

"Radio City? What's that?"

"It's almost done, and it's just the most gigantic theater. The place looks swell, so big. They're calling it the 'People's Showplace.' But the ticket takers and ushers will wear these funny red suits and little caps. That's what I feel like."

"Well, I think you look damn cute, toots, and—"

Ann heard the sound of steps outside, more than one person.

"Hey sounds like we got company."

"Susan?" Ann said. "Coming back?"

"Could be, and someone else."

The steps grew closer and then the sound of a key in the lock, and the door opened.

And Ann's roommate walked in, followed by a tall man in a bowler, with thick dark eyebrows and a half-lit cigar in his mouth.

He shut the door behind him. "Where's your toilet, ladies? I gotta go something bad."

"Late night?" Ellie said to Susan.

"Uh-huh, and I'm not sure it's over," the other girl said. Susan wore a lot of makeup, Ann thought, ruby red lips, a powdery pink blush to her cheeks, dark mascara. She was easily five years older, Ann guessed . . . maybe more. An aging flapper.

"So you the new girl?"

Ann nodded as Susan stuck out her hand.

"Nice to meet you, kid. I just had to bring Johnny up, you know, to use the facilities."

"Missed work today?" Ellie said, taking a sip of the gin.

"Nah, did a switch with one of the other girls. Got five days of straight hoofing ahead of me." Susan grabbed a glass and poured some gin. "You a dancer too?" she said to Ann.

Ann told her about the diving bell, and that made Susan laugh. "Show business, hm? You never know where you'll end up."

Then her boyfriend came out.

"So . . . great. I gotta go, Susie. But hey look—"

And in that moment Johnny looked down to Ann with predatory eyes that made even the stares and leers of agents look like nothing in comparison.

"This Friday, we got a band, a singer. Going to be dancing. All three of you should come." He glanced away from Ann, but then went right back to her. "Gonna be my treat, okay?"

Ann looked at Ellie. It was clear who and what Johnny was. Ellie shot Ann a quick look as if to say . . . *Don't say anything.*

"Maybe. Maybe we can."

Johnny smiled. "I won't take no for an answer, pretty ladies. Besides, free booze, free food . . ." He looked knowingly at Susan. "And I know you girls don't make that much."

"Okay," Ellie answered, "we'll try to come."

Johnny took a step to Ann. The guy was not only tall, but broad, like somebody who lifted heavy things a lot. "You too, toots?"

"Sure. I'll try."

The man smiled, held his glance for a second.

"I gotta go."

And instead of a good-bye kiss to Susan, who appeared to be his girlfriend, he gave her a pat on her rump. Then he sailed out of the small apartment.

"Well," Ellie said, "guess we all know what we're doing Friday night?"

She tapped out a cigarette, lit it, and sent a circle of smoke up to the ceiling of the dingy kitchen.

"Could be fun," Susan said.

And Ann wondered, and not for the first time that day, why she felt as if she was drifting, sailing toward something that wasn't under her control.

The strange, the unknown, the surprising.

And after meeting Johnny, she wondered whether she should add one other possibility . . .

The dangerous.

20

Halifax, Nova Scotia

CARL DENHAM LOOKED OUT THE hospital window. He could see the *Venture* moored next to a line of freighters, dwarfed by them.

Halifax harbor.

Not exactly at the top of his destination wish lists.

And they'd be there for a while . . . weeks maybe. He already told Englehorn back on the ship that they weren't leaving until Herb was ready to travel.

"I'll eat the cost. The production will eat it. I'm staying till he can go home, skipper," he had said.

And the captain knew better than to argue with him.

But now, looking at the *Venture* in its freight ship sandwich, looking drab, small by comparison, Denham had to wonder.

Can I really afford this?

Got a star, or an actor at any rate, on board doing nothing but hitting the Halifax gin mills. Got a crew edgy, wanting to be doing something. The clock was ticking, and the goddamn meter too.

And what did Denham have to show for it? Some

footage of the sea, shots of the actor climbing rocks, and maybe—when it's developed—some great stuff that Herb shot before he was attacked.

Maybe.

Not much, certainly not a movie. And he had promised Herb that as soon as he was ready to travel, he'd take him back to New York City himself.

Told him that, as they pushed the *Venture*'s engines as fast as they could go racing to Halifax and the hospital.

Now he waited . . . with Hayes in a chair, head thrown back, sleeping. The hero of the day if there ever was one. Denham promised himself not to forget that.

Englehorn would be coming here soon.

To hear the news.

None of them bothered to lie to Herb on the ship. No one told him, *Hell, it's okay kid. Your leg is going to be fine. You're going to be all right.*

A door opened behind Denham, and the doctor came out.

Immediately, Denham could see from the man's face—the dark circles, the bags under his eyes—that he had been working hard doing some grim task.

"Okay, you are Carl Denham? His boss?"

Carl nodded. Hayes stirred awake, rubbed his eyes and stood up.

"Okay, then, let me tell you what we've done, and what will have to be done."

"Okay, Doc. Let's hear it."

"The leg has suffered multiple tears just under the

knee, broken bone, torn muscle and ligament. There wasn't much it was hanging by. And above the knee, nasty damage there too, big gashes. How many animals did he have on him?"

Hayes answered the question. "It was hard to see, Doctor. But I killed four of them all round him. More may have scattered after the gunshots."

"God." The doctor took a breath. "We had to remove his leg, and quickly. He lost a lot of blood, plus the danger of infection from a wound of that size. I mean, he's lucky he didn't die."

"So it's done?" Denham said.

"That part. Wound bandaged. We did . . . a good job."

Hayes spoke again. "And now?"

"Now? He has to get better. Then, there are possibilities."

"You mean stay here?" Denham said.

"Yes. A week or two before you can move him anywhere. That is, if you want to move him. But since you're heading to New York, you should take him there. They got the best people . . ."

"People. For what?"

"Prosthetics. With the right prosthetic, your friend can walk again. Will take time. Months maybe. Getting stronger, learning how to walk on it. But he can do it."

For the first time since the attack, Denham smiled.

"Great. I mean, he'll walk. He can have his life."

"Guess you could say that. He'll need help. Money for the prosthetic, of course—"

"No problem."

"And someone to stand by him, help him, encourage him. Something a bit more than just a friend."

"Don't worry, Doc. I'll do that."

"Okay then. Well, if you want to wait a bit, I can let you see him. Groggy from the morphine. But, you'll be able to talk."

And impulsively, Denham reached out and clapped the doctor on the back.

Denham and Hayes, now joined by Englehorn, entered the dimly lit hospital room.

He saw Herb on the bed, eyes shut. Denham stopped.

"Maybe," he whispered, "we should come back la—"

But Herb's eyes shot open, and the camera operator turned to face them.

"Hey," he said in a heavy voice, the voice thin.

Denham walked over to the bed.

"Herb, how you doing, pal?"

As soon as he said it, Denham realized it was a stupid question. *How the hell do you think he's doing?*

"No surprises, eh, guys? Lost the right one. Though, funny thing, can't feel it gone. Like it's still there."

Both Hayes and Englehorn seemed tongue-tied.

Denham continued: "Now, don't you worry, Herb. As soon as you can travel, we head to New York. The doc says there are some swell prosthetics—you know, artificial—legs they can fit you up with. In months, you'll be back turning the crank."

The man's eyes lowered.

Maybe, Denham thought, *he doesn't believe me.*

"Carl, you got to go back. Shoot some film. You can't afford—"

"Don't tell me what I can afford. What kind of director would I be without my cameraman? Maybe we'll be able to shoot some stuff around here, you know, around Halifax."

Herb made a small laugh.

"That would be"—he coughed—"a different movie."

"Anyway, don't you worry about it. You get better, then we head back to New York City. Understand?"

Herb nodded. The he craned his neck around, to see Hayes, standing to the side.

"You know, I'd be dead if not for you."

"Don't worry about—"

"No, listen, Hayes. You saved my life. Thank God for your aim. You saved my life. And I won't ever forget that."

Denham looked at Hayes. Usually the mate didn't say a lot; one of those people who kept things bottled up. But now Hayes leaned forward and put a hand on Herb's shoulder.

"My pleasure, Herb. You don't owe me anything."

Herb's hand went up to Hayes and gave it a pat.

"I think we better get back to the ship," Englehorn said. "He looks tired."

"Yeah," Denham said. "We'll check in on you. Every day. Till we leave the wonderful city of Halifax."

Herb smiled, already closing his eyes.

"Good . . ."

Then shut. Englehorn nodded to him that it was time.

Until we leave Halifax . . . Denham thought.

Leave it for what?

That was the interesting thing about the future. You could plan it, you could think about it, even imagine it.

But what would it be?

Ah, that was the trick. Like some kind of leering carnival barker hawking a ten-in-one show. Want to see the future, rube? You just gotta go there . . . to really know what it is.

They walked out of the room, out of the small hospital, and out to the street, now dark, the streetlamps flickering to life.

Denham turned to the others.

"I'm going to wire New York. Let them know what happened, what we're doing . . . see you back on the boat."

"All right, Denham," Englehorn said.

Yup, Denham thought as they walked away. *Wire New York, and maybe walk around and try to think what the hell I'm going to do now.*

21

San Francisco

"WHERE'S THE SHIP, TOMMY? I don't see—"

"Down there, Lieutenant—sorry, I will really *try* to stop that."

Sam turned to the young former gob. "No Tommy, you *will* stop it. You will, or I'm not sailing or diving or doing anything with you constantly reminding me that I used to be a naval officer and now God knows what I am."

"You're a diver!" Tommy laughed.

"Oh, that's what I am? I thought I was just another unemployed soon-to-be bum. But where the hell is the ship?"

Tommy pointed at the far end of the docks, past a row of piers, some with freighters waiting.

"Down there. You can't see it because of the big ship. Come on. The captain is waiting for you."

Tommy led the way, walking fast. The brilliant morning sunlight glistened on the water of the harbor. If Sam really took this job, he'd miss San Francisco.

Tommy was ahead of him now, nearly running. He

turned back to Sam. "There she is, you can see her now!"

Sam couldn't see anything, but then a few feet more, he saw . . . the ship.

A boat. An almost funny-looking, half-tug, half-trawler boat. The kid couldn't be serious. . . .

The boat had a hoist arm, and even from here Sam could see the diving compressor sitting squat on the rear of the boat.

Well, thought Sam, *this is as good a way to die as any.* . . .

Tommy jumped onto the ship near a dark-haired man, cigarette stuck in his mouth, hosing down the ship.

"We're here to see Captain Rosa," Tommy said, shooting Sam a grin. The crewman nodded in the direction of the wheelhouse.

Sam thought: *I could just turn and walk away from this ship.*

He half expected Popeye the sailor to emerge from what passed as a bridge that looked like a wooden closet attached to the mast.

"Captain R——" Tommy started.

But then he appeared, the captain. Bald head, skin the color of leather, a dark mustache. He could have been thirty; he could have been sixty.

"Hey, you, who gave you permission to come onto my ship?"

"Captain, it's me. We talked yesterday and this——"

"Oh, right. You the kid, the baby diver."

The crewman hosing the deck snickered at that.

"Th—this is the master diver I told you about."

Tommy gestured at Sam. Captain Rosa looked up, and his equally dark eyes studied Sam.

Then he nodded.

"Okay then, the two of you come aboard."

Aye, aye . . . thought Sam. *The guy must think he captained the* Queen Elizabeth.

Sam went close to the boat. The crewman looked up. Sam nodded, then jumped onto the deck.

Captain Rosa walked down three steps to the deck.

"Luis Rosa, captain of the *Susana*." He stuck his hand out warily. Sam shook it.

"Sam Kelly."

Rosa squeezed Sam's hand as if to prove something. Sam gave back as good as he got, all the time not showing any sign of discomfort.

"Captain Kelly, from the, er, Navy?"

Sam looked at Tommy, who shrugged, indicating the increase in Sam's rank wasn't his fault.

"Lieutenant Kelly, Captain. Ex-Navy. Unemployed."

Rosa's face was set, stonelike. No expression. Sam had met Portuguese fishermen in Sheepshead Bay. Strong characters, strong fishermen . . . real sea men.

And Rosa seemed as strong and as strange as any he had met.

"Okay . . . ex-Navy. But not an ex-diver, eh?"

"A diver looking for diving work."

"This, the *Mia Susana,* is a dive ship. Tough little ship. A hardworking diver ship."

"If you say so."

The humor didn't land to good effect, Sam guessed from the subtle squinting of Rosa's eyes.

"Two of my divers, they get arrested. Drunk. Knives. Who knows when they get out! I have one diver, but not enough. We work hard. And I need to go. Make money."

"You need divers."

Now a hint of smile at the corners of Rosa's mouth.

"You ever dive for pearls?"

"No."

"I can train. Just like any deep diving, only you can find a real treasure . . . pearls. The right pearls, and we all do okay, hm?" A bigger smile. "You interested?"

"Sure."

"Good, I hire you then."

"Hey, wait a minute," Tommy said. "I said, it was the two of us, and I—"

Rosa held up a hand.

"I don't need two more divers. One good diver"—a look right at Sam—"one more great diver is enough. I hire just him."

A finger jab at Sam.

He looked at Tommy, who saw his dream of adventure and wealth vanishing.

"Too bad," Sam said.

"Hm?"

"He doesn't go, I don't go. He brought me here, after all."

Hesitation then. Rosa looking everywhere but at Sam and Tommy.

Then he looked up.

"You're right. He did. Okay, the two of you . . . the baby diver . . . and a real diver, eh?"

He stuck out his hand.

Sam took it and shook it, and he saw Tommy on the side grinning like a kid.

Rosa gave them a quick tour of the small boat. The room with the dive gear, which actually looked well maintained. A bunk room where they'd all sleep. Something resembling a mess—but would hardly hold more than two people eating at a time.

The rest of the crew would be boarding by sunset for next morning's sail.

Sam could get his stuff—some of it anyway, maybe a few books to read.

When they got back on the deck, he checked the compressor. Not as new as Sam would have liked, but like the gear below, it looked well maintained. No sign of rust, the metal shiny, cleaned of salt and corrosion. First dive out would tell if looks were deceiving or not.

"So," Rosa said, "you understand the split, eh? One-third to me, one-third to you divers, and one-third for the rest of the crew."

The sun was higher in the sky, and what was left of a morning chill had vanished.

Sam turned to the captain. "And where do we sail to . . ."

Another small smile. "Did I ask something humorous?" Sam remarked.

Rosa raised a finger, delivering the first of what Sam guessed would be many lectures by the captain.

"No captain of a pearl ship would ever—ever!—tell where they go. We sail, you dive, and—"

"Then I guess you go, I don't—"

Sam made to turn away. He saw a horrified look on Tommy's face.

Rosa blinked. Another characteristic of the good captain that he'd have to remember.

"Okay. I can tell you some."

"Tell me then."

Rosa leaned close. "A spot in the Indian Ocean. Not too deep. Good for big pearls. But far west from Sumatra."

"The kid told me near Sumatra . . . hoped to do some sight-seeing."

Rosa shook his head.

"Some islands nearby . . . who knows. But we will be in"—he tapped his bald head—"someplace secret."

"Well, I guess the Indian Ocean . . . is a bit of a destination."

Rosa smiled. "Yes. And don't worry, my diver friend, I will make sure you have adventures, if not on Sumatra, then other places. Is a big world, no?"

"So I've heard."

"Good. We sail at morning!"

And Rosa bounded back to his bridge, while Tommy jumped off the boat, followed by Sam.

Walking back to the hotel, Tommy turned to Sam.

"Hey, Sam, thanks."

"What for?"

"Back there. I mean, he didn't really want me—"

"No kidding."

"But you got me on. I'm part of the dive team."

"You're a diver, aren't you? You got me the job. And a job is a good thing to have these days."

"I owe you. Twice now. And I always pay my debts."

"No debt. But you watch my back down there, and I'll watch yours, okay?"

"Of course."

They had reached the top of the hill. From here they could see San Francisco below them, the water in the distance.

Soon there would be a massive bridge to cross that bay. Starting early next year, Sam had read.

The world is changing.

Growing smaller.

Good time to have an adventure, somewhere in the Indian Ocean. The days of adventure in the big wide world might be numbered.

He turned to Tommy.

"Let's celebrate, kid. How about we find a place that will sell us an illegal beer or two?"

Tommy grinned as though it might have been Christmas . . . and Sam led the way to the speakeasy near his hotel.

Morning, as he well knew, would come soon enough. . . .

BOOK TWO
The Discovery
1932

22

On an uncharted island,
somewhere in the Indian Ocean

THE POUNDING OF THE DRUMS, the chanting, the yelling filled the night air.

Flickering torches surrounded a young girl, the flames that seemed to move in time to the chants, to the endless pounding.

An old woman gave her something to drink; the girl shook her head, but the woman grabbed the girl's head and forced her . . . to drink.

The young girl swallowed some, then spit out the rest. Then she opened her mouth, trying to say something, trying to beg.

Her throat sounded raw, rough, worn to a raspy brittle sound from so much pleading, so much begging.

Then the girl looked around at everyone, all staring at her. Their eyes wide watching this girl's struggle.

She tried to move her arms, but heavy ropes kept her wrists firmly pinned.

She looked back and forth at her tiny arms, her small hands, clenched so tight.

Now the ropes began to move. She began to rise, over the pounding, the flickering torches everywhere. As the streams of burning oil ran down the wall, the streams blurring together, dizzying runnels of fire . . .

She shook—her body shivering, wriggling as she dangled, and they raised her high, higher . . . to her fate.

To her doom.

It began when the island shook. The island *shook,* rocking the huts, sending young children falling to the sand.

A warning and a demand.

And now it was time to give someone to . . . Kong.

Others huddled quietly in their huts, the ones who were safe. They would hear the pounding drums, the strange words. Only waiting until it was over, and peace would return.

Then today, the choosing began.

All the women of the village standing, waiting.

And the strange woman looked at the line of young women, searching for the right one.

Then—suddenly—the old woman walked to this young girl, and with a single simple gesture it was done.

They took her. And the day of horror began, which would lead inevitably to a night even more unimaginable.

They moved her closer, this dangling girl, right to the stone wall, to the mammoth barrier.

Sloping up, curving in. This wall that protected them, this wall that *separated* them. The giant stone faces looked at her, so much larger than a person, terrifying in their strange, twisting faces. The wall was now so close that the girl could almost touch it—if her hands were free. The torches below became smaller, the men all looking up, the sound of their chanting finally fading.

The girl's eyes closed for a moment; the drink they gave her made it hard to keep her eyes open.

And one word rose above all others, clear, loud— *Kong!*

Then over and over . . . *Kong . . . Kong . . . Kong.*

No girl ever went to the other side of the wall and returned. And for the others, life on the other side of the wall would continue—until once more the island shook, and it would all begin again.

Kong . . . Kong . . . Kong!

And then the pallet stopped and the girl stopped going up. New sounds now—noises, ropes and wood being moved. Her body shook crazily, rocking left and right, but still suspended.

Until, the rocking stopped, and then the pallet started *down* slowly.

Her descending body passed the leaders gathered on the wall, looking at her, their mouths bellowing the ancient words. Chanting so loudly as if that might hurry the pallet on its way.

Down, now on the other side of the wall. The only light, faint, barely reaching down to the chasm . . . the torches atop the wall. The lights from the village completely cut off, vanished. The sound of the villagers now muffled, cut off by the massive wall.

And then she looked in the other direction.

Into the darkness of the island, the hidden jungle with its mountains, and trees, and secrets.

Some of the nearby trees and giant vines caught the scant light. But beyond them, nothing of the dark, almost black jungle was visible.

They kept lowering her, the men above her watching, studying her dangling body, its steady fall.

Until—it finally came to a halt.

She was on ground, on a stone platform, suspended near the edge of the black jungle. Nothing visible to her but the horrible wall on one side, and the terrible darkness on the other.

When suddenly the chanting, the drums, *stopped*.

The old woman appeared atop the wall and said more words. Then all was quiet. The girl turned as if cocking her ears, as if . . . listening for sounds close by, sounds from those trees, from the towering plants.

Sounds that might be close to her.

Then from above, that single word again from the woman, her voice so strong.

Kong!

Followed by a sound that dwarfed all others, the low rumble of a giant metal gong, smashed, once, then again, then again . . .

Silence.

The girl's head turned again, facing the jungle.

She was breathing fast, the air bellowing in and out, as if trying to store oxygen for whatever would happen next.

Silence.

Then, in the distance, clearly from so far away. Far away, yet, deep, powerful.

A roar. In answer.

It was coming.

Kong was coming.

Another roar, and even in those few moments, it grew clearer, louder.

Coming here.

The girl screamed then, and looked up at her clenched fists. The rough ropes binding her had rubbed her skin raw.

Another roar.

Something close by moved—a new sound . . . the rustle of brush, plants. Something not small at all, but moving, *running* from that noise.

The girl closed her eyes.

Kong would soon be here.

23

25 degrees, 30 minutes, 44 degrees, 5 minutes—
The Indian Ocean

SAM KELLY POPPED TO THE surface to see that the sky had turned a deep blue. The sun, blocked by the *Mia Susana*, outlined the ship with a fiery orange.

He grabbed the hoist, and waited while they used it to raise his now-dead weight out of the water.

With each few feet, the glow grew more brilliant until, completely out, he could see the setting sun, making the ocean appear on fire.

Beautiful, Sam thought. *So beautiful.*

And below? A reef unlike anything he had ever seen, a forest of twisting coral; the oyster beds with their pearls protected by towering fortresses of coral.

Incredible.

And the fish . . . Sam didn't know such colors existed, let alone the number of fish he had seen.

They moved Sam onto the deck and lowered him down into a chair. Two of the crewmen quickly started undoing the bolts that fastened his helmet. Another removed the lead yoke, the heavy weight that lay on his shoulders.

Tommy took off the helmet.

"Just in time for dinner, Sam."

Sam smiled. The two of them were on their own on this ship. A few of the crew spoke no English and stayed to themselves. The others did their job and tried to stay out of Captain Rosa's way.

Then there was Dr. Bakali.

There was a third diver, who for some reason was called Dr. Bakali; Sam guessed there was some kind of grim joke attached to the name. He and Rosa were clearly friends, and Bakali made no secret that he didn't think much of the two inexperienced pearl divers.

Though once Sam showed that there wasn't anything about helmet diving he didn't know, Bakali backed off.

Still, he always had something to say.

"Not much down there, eh?" Bakali said, squatting close to Sam, a stub of cigar in his mouth. The smell of the cigar, after breathing the compressed air, made Sam's stomach go tight.

As though Bakali knew it did exactly that.

Bakali patted Sam's shoulder. "You know, it's like I tell Rosa. You may know diving, but finding the beds, looking for the right oysters. We are"—he laughed, exaggeratedly loud in front of Sam's face—"a pearl ship, eh?"

Bakali stood up. "Some things take experience, hm, *amigo*?"

Sam stood up so they could pull off the dive suit.

This was like being a matador, ready to face some underwater bull. And the razor-sharp coral, some shaped like horns, could easily gore you.

Tommy leaned close. "That guy never lets up."

"I've noticed."

Bakali could be especially cruel to Tommy . . . to the point that Sam was thinking that sooner or later, they would have to have words about it.

Or maybe not . . . words.

The ship cook, Jorge—who also served Rosa in at least three other roles on the ship—stuck his head out from below.

"You want to eat, you eat now."

"Guess he means dinner is served," Sam said.

Tommy grinned, and followed him below to the cramped mess room.

Rosa gestured with his knife. "We Portuguese ruled the oceans, eh? Our ships were the fastest. Our captains the best. We sailed around the globe when your people"—he winked at Bakali, then looked back to Sam—"were figuring out new things to do with potatoes."

Sam grinned. The nightly lectures were something Sam had gotten used to. To be on this ship was to enroll in a class on Portugal's incredible, and to Rosa, neglected, place in history.

"Captain . . ." It was Ernesto, who functioned as more or less a first mate. The Basque had perpetual bags under his eyes, and his stringy hair looked as though it had never had an encounter with a comb. Ernesto didn't say much. So . . . this was unusual.

"What, what do you want?" Rosa looked at Sam again. "The Basques! Takes them forever to get a sentence out." Back to Ernesto. "What the hell do you want?"

The other table of crewmen lowered their voices, probably eager to hear what the tongue-tied Spaniard had to say.

Jorge plopped down another bowl of what looked like cabbage and meat floating in a thin, watery sauce. The food here was easily a notch or two below Navy fare.

"Every day," Ernesto began, "we sail further west. Away from Sumatra." The first mate shrugged. "Why?"

Rosa laughed.

"He asks why. My Basque *amigo* asks his captain *why*. Okay, I will tell you."

Now the crew at the other table became completely silent. Here was a subject that interested them all. Tommy looked at Sam.

Rosa stood up.

"You see how we do here. Yes, we get some pearls, but so many of these beds, off the islands, in the shallows . . . they are not the way they used to be. Other boats come, the oyster beds change."

"So why . . . west? There's nothing there. Just the sea," Ernesto asked.

Rosa made a condescending smile. "So, what do you

think I do when we are inshore, when everyone has a good time, spend their money like fools, hm?"

He didn't wait for an answer.

"I will tell you. I talk to the other captains, and not just the pearl boats, but the big fishing boats, even the freighters carrying who knows what . . . from China to California. And I begin to see something." He tapped his head. "I begin to understand something. I am Portuguese. Sailing is in my blood, no?"

"What is it you understand, Captain?" Ernesto said.

"That we think we know so much about the sea; we think we know it all. But it is so big. If a place wasn't in the fishing currents, or used for trade, then there should be so much we don't know. Islands, great reefs, whole sections ripe to be discovered. Quietly, secretly! To look for pearls where no one ever has."

Sam cleared his throat. He was only a diver, perhaps below—in the pecking order—even the first mate. "And if you find nothing?"

Rosa turned to Sam. Everyone knew he had been in the Navy; maybe they weren't surprised that he would question Rosa. At any rate, Rosa nodded, and took a few moments before responding.

"Of course. Yes, we could find nothing. Just great stretches of Pacific, remote, endless. That could happen. But listen to me, my ex-lieutenant, without going somewhere new, somewhere people have not gone before, then we know—we *know*—we will find only what they found, to dive only where others have dived. It's my ship. My chance. My decision."

"Captain." It was Ernesto again. Sam expected another challenge.

But the sad-eyed Basque looked up. "Thank you for telling me, telling us. Now at least we know what we are doing."

The challenge was over. Now onward to parts unknown, on a small dive boat with a captain who relived the dream days of the great Portuguese navigators.

And not for the first time, Sam had to wonder . . .

What the hell am I doing here?

24

On an uncharted island

THE GROUND SHOOK.

And with the shaking, the noise of every massive step, cutting through the jungle, as if the creature's rage, its bellow alone could clear a path, the terrible roar itself powerful enough.

The villagers, safe on the wall, still cringed as they looked down at her, waiting, watching, safe. Her screams grew even more ragged now.

Pound . . . pound . . . pound . . . and then a new sound, the snapping of trees being pushed away, snapped like twigs.

The power immense, overwhelming.

And the girl—so young, small, and slender—looked into the darkness, alone, facing what was coming for her.

But this girl had watched things; she had tried to figure out things.

Things like what had happened on this island . . . what could the wall possibly mean? No one ever talked to her about it.

But she looked at what was done.

She looked—and thought about death . . . and Kong.

And she must have thought about other things, maybe sneaking a look at one of the women before her, sailing high up to the wall top, then over.

How to escape? What could one do? Was there *anything* one could do?

Resist the heavy ropes. Heavy and thick—because of . . . Kong?

Did she think that maybe there might be something that could be done there?

Then she must have had an idea. She must have thought that if she could keep some control, then maybe there might be a way to escape.

If she escaped, the leaders would kill her.

She could never go back to the village.

That was impossible.

There would be only one way . . . deeper into the island, to its secrets, its dangers.

She would have no choice.

More trees *snapping,* the wood now so like the explosions that roared from the sky, or the even worse explosions that erupted from the mountain when the island shook.

If the girl was going to act, she had to act now.

The leaders on the wall watched her below.

Not one of them would guess what she was about to do now.

What she had planned.

Her fists tight, and in each, a rolled piece of cloth, filled with grease taken from the meals.

She squeezed hard. She looked at her hands, the grease gathered from the wooden plates oozing out between her fingers.

A big dollop fell onto the ground, useless.

A giant snap of wood, and she looked up. Her plan wasn't working; a foolish idea, and now Kong was so close. Another roar, the ground shaking, trembling.

But then a trail of watery grease streamed down one hand, then the other, down to her wrists, her small girl's wrists, so thin.

Creeping, so slowly, too slowly.

She turned back to the dark jungle; and something *moved* there.

She had only seconds.

The grease hit both wrists. Furiously the girl twisted her arms, back and forth, crazy, faster, the rope cutting her wrists, and then—

When the grease had spread all around, she tugged.

As she tugged, both her hands caught right below the thumb; but she quickly forced her fingers together, each hand doing the same things as she jerked, and pulled, and tugged, until—

One hand popped *free,* timed to another roar loud enough to hurt her ears.

And if the other remained stuck? Then it would be useless. There would not be enough time.

Tugging harder, steady, tugging and—

Until that hand too popped free.

And Kong had to be only seconds away from breaking through the brush, to get to the wall.

Some of the darkness in the jungle seemed to move; he was there.

She jumped off the stone, onto the ramp that led into the jungle.

An opening in the dense wall of green lay to the side, a place between two towering trees where the vines and plants weren't so thick.

The girl started running, not looking back, tripping, getting up, running as fast as she could.

Another roar, and for the first time that night, this night of horror, the roar sounded farther away.

Even as it was constant now.

He was there. He found the empty stone, the heavy ropes scented by the grease of cooked animals.

The nightmare had only begun.

But the girl was still alive . . . and on the run.

25

New York City

CARL DENHAM HOPPED OUT OF the cab, hurrying through a New York downpour, the rain coming down as though someone had turned on a gigantic faucet over the city.

In a minute he was soaked, even just dashing to the door of "21."

He knocked, and the doorman let him in, smiling.

"Evening, Mr. Denham. Nasty out tonight, hm?"

Denham hurried past the doorman. "New York weather. You gotta love it."

"Mr. Driscoll is waiting for you in the back, with a guest."

Guest? Strange, when they arranged this meeting up for a drink, Carl thought it would be just the two of them. A good chance for them to catch up. Traveling with a crew who didn't think much about anything, Denham could use a dose of Driscoll's wit.

And what better place than "21"—though in reality the establishment was an illegal speakeasy, Prohibition was just about ignored in Manhattan.

Thousands of years of human beings enjoying a beer

or a shot of whiskey, and some crazy people thought a law would change that.

Instead, it became a damn field day for the gangsters. Denham had already watched them muscle into the picture business, funneling some of their booze money into something legit.

He guessed it would take decades undoing the damage—that is if the damage could be undone.

He moved through a sea of tables, lit by candles, the jewelry on some of the Broadway babes making the room glitter.

What a great place! If Carl couldn't be out at sea, going somewhere exotic, shooting something, then this was as close to heaven as could be.

He saw Jack Driscoll, and next to him a guy with a mustache, wavy hair—Irish-looking, and somewhat familiar.

"Jack, have you seen what it's doing out there? I'm soaked."

Driscoll stubbed out his cigarette.

"Heard some thunder before. Have a seat; your first martini's on me."

Denham nodded, and he took a free place.

"I want to introduce a friend of mine . . . Eugene O'Neill."

The other man stuck out his hand. "Gene."

"Carl Denham," Denham said.

He saw Jack shoot a look at the other man as though they were on the inside of some top-secret joke.

Jack leaned over. "Gene's a writer."

"Ah, another struggling *artiste*? Tough business, even for Jack who is damn good."

Jack laughed, while his friend reached for a pack of Pall Mall. Tapped one out, and lit up.

"Carl, Gene is a lot more successful than I am. You never heard of him?"

"You know me. Not a lot of time to hit the Great White Way. I barely get to see *your* plays."

"In fact, you don't. You missed the last two."

"Bad timing, kiddo, and besides they didn't stay open long enough. Like I said, tough business."

Then the other man spoke.

"And what is it you do, Mr. Denham?"

"Carl, Gene, *Carl*. Or if you ever work for me, call me 'Denham.' " Denham laughed. "Been a long time since I've been a Mister anything. I make movies."

"Film? Interesting. There are plans to film one of my plays."

"Really? Then you must be doing okay."

Jack laughed aloud. "Carl, this is Eugene O'Neill, award-winning, successful playwright. Everyone knows him."

It was O'Neill's turn to laugh.

"Obviously not everyone."

"Like I said. I don't get out much. Usually running around looking for money." Then to Jack. "Like now."

Then back to O'Neill.

"So what do you write? Musicals?"

"Never did that. Usually write drama. Serious stuff."

Between puffs, O'Neill smiled. "Maybe too serious. But you know—I am working on a comedy now."

"You're kidding?" Jack said.

"Not at all. All about my youth, filtered through some happier glass. Maybe . . . one of these." He tilted his own martini glass. "A real comedy. And you know, I think it's pretty good."

"I can't believe it," Jack said. He turned back to Denham. "Gene wrote *Mourning Becomes Electra*."

"Hey, I did hear about that. Something to do with the Greek tragedy?"

O'Neill grinned. "You could say that . . . I stole a bit from Orestes, and transplanted it to the post–Civil War New England. Guess I turned it into an American tragedy."

"Now *that's* a good title."

"You really should read a paper now and then, Carl." Jack raised his hand to a waiter.

"Try getting the *Herald Tribune* delivered in the Arctic, Jack. It's a problem."

"Another?" Jack said to O'Neill.

"Love to, Jack. You know me. But I've promised to meet the wife for dinner. One more of these, and I'm sure I'll start to think of better things to do."

O'Neill stood up.

"Next time, dinner? Love to read *Ah, Wilderness!* when it's ready."

Denham watched Gene shake Jack's hand strongly. "You'll be among the first." He turned to Denham.

"And nice to meet you, Carl. Good luck with your photoplays."

Carl shook the writer's hand.

Then Eugene O'Neill sailed out of the club slowly, almost—Denham thought—as if reluctant to leave the flickering warmth, or the booze, or the camaraderie.

"So he's famous?"

Jack ginned. "Very. He's a genius. The best we have. I'll never be that good. Never."

"Hey, don't put yourself down. You'll be—"

The waiter arrived with two martinis—Denham's first and a refill for his friend.

"You were saying?"

"Oh right—sure you will be. You're brilliant."

"If you say so. . . ." Another sip. "How's Herb?"

"Doing great. Gotta tell you, even the doctors at Columbia Presbyterian were impressed with what they did up there in Nova Scotia. And they have him walking—can you imagine that?—walking on the prosthetic. They say he'll be ready to do whatever he wants to do in a few weeks."

"So you got your cameraman back?"

"Yeah. He was crazy to go for that shot."

"People like to please you, Carl. That's what you . . . bring out. They want to make you happy. Even if it means getting attacked by a hundred sea lions."

"It wasn't a hundred, and they were seals."

"Thank God for Hayes."

"Amen to that." Denham took a sip. A perfectly chilled martini, flecks of ice floating on the surface. Heaven. "And how's your new play going?"

"It's going. Slow, steady—I'm the tortoise of playwrights. But—I dunno—having trouble with the romance that drives the whole story. It's like I don't know what the guy should say."

"Now I wonder why that is?"

"Funny."

"I mean, I make movies about dangerous places and exotic animals. Because that's what I know, got it? How could you write about romance without having had much experience . . ."

"I've dated."

"Yeah, and I've passed by a church once too. About as frequently."

Jack looked uncomfortable. Denham knew someone would nail him. Jack Driscoll would lose his heart big time. He'd fall like someone jumping off a building.

"And what about you?"

"Me? Romance? I'm a filmmaker, Jack. Filmmakers have no time for—"

Jack laughed again, an infectious sound, warm, genuine. Denham always felt smarter, wittier with his friend. It was a good feeling.

"No, your next steps, plans?"

"Oh, that . . ." Another icy sip. "I'm working a few angles. The investors weren't happy. So they cooked up a compromise."

"To make up for the money, for the lost expedition?"

"Yeah. A jungle picture. We're going to meet about it in a few days."

"Now that is funny. And you're going to do it?"

"Have to. And here's the worst part—they got Bruce Baxter for the lead."

"Oh. Lucky you."

"Right. If only he had a brain cell."

"Women seem to like him. Any female lead?"

"They're looking. That part will come later."

"And your locations, treks to real jungles?"

Denham leaned close. "Budget's tight. But I know my way around budgets. I've built enough in, but cutting corners that I can take the *Venture* out . . . once I figure where to go. Just need one thing . . ."

Denham fixed his eyes on Jack.

"Let me guess—it has something to do with me."

"Yes. I need a story, Jack. Just the start for now, stuff we can start in a studio for now. You can turn in the script for jungle stuff later."

"Carl, I can't. I'm buried with this new work. We have a producer's reading in a few weeks."

Denham clasped his friend's forearm.

"I don't need the whole thing, kiddo. Just enough to get the thing rolling, keep the moneymen happy . . . while I start thinking where we can shoot the real jungle stuff. Thinking an island, maybe."

"Caribbean?"

"Nah, something new. Something people haven't seen. Still working on that. But Jack, you got to help me."

"For free . . . ?"

"You'll get paid—eventually. You know me."

"Yeah, that's part of the problem."

"You'll get paid. Just give me enough to get Baxter and some of the other actors busy. We'll get a girl, then the real story. You can do it."

"Yeah, but do I want to?"

"It's for me . . . how can you say no?"

Jack downed his martini. "Right, how *could* I. And now, I think I need another."

Denham sat back.

He was almost back in business—and that was cause enough to celebrate.

26

The Indian Ocean

SAM WATCHED THE SURFACE OF the turquoise blue water break as Tommy's helmet popped up. Then the diver's hand reached above his helmet, thumb straight up.

I trained the kid good, Sam thought. A smart diver. Though there was one thing he couldn't give the kid, and that was experience. Tommy needed a lot of dives under his belt before he got to that point where when something went wrong—and something sooner or later always went wrong—he'd be calm as can be.

The kid did fine being trapped on the training wreck. But what would happen here, out in the open water?

Panic was the killer. Every helmet diver knew that. Getting twisted up in your own air tubes, stumbling, turning, forgetting where the release valve was, letting the air build up in a suit . . .

It could all happen so fast.

The crew pulled Tommy to the metal platform to raise him out of the water. One of them shouted an order in Portuguese, and the platform started coming up, the water cascading off Tommy.

Captain Rosa stood outside the wheelhouse talking to Bakali.

Both looked grim, faces set.

And the reason was clear. Tommy had sent up only a few pearls. Barely worth the time sending him down.

If there was some secret, unknown place where oysters would be found, they had yet to stumble upon it. And Sam knew they were hundreds of miles from any shipping lanes, far from any place where other vessels had gone for pearls.

"God, Sam—it's **beautiful down there.**"

Tommy was oblivious of the mood on the ship. Sam guessed he better have a talk with him.

Too much cheeriness could be a problem.

"Yeah, kid, when you're out of your suit, come on the stern deck. We need a little chat."

Tommy's smile faded a bit, the lightbulb finally coming on.

Tommy had a cigarette between his lips.

"Divers don't smoke," Sam said.

Tommy took another drag. Looked at the cigarette and flicked it over the side.

"You're the instructor."

"Ex-instructor. It's just that you need your lungs in the best shape possible."

"But aren't smokes supposed to be good for coughs, and—"

Sam laughed. "Guess you believe everything you read?"

"No. Not really."

The engine started up, and the deck below them began to vibrate. Sam heard the anchor chain being pulled up.

"We're moving," Tommy said. "Where we going?"

"Beats me. Cap'n Rosa has not chosen to confide in me. But my guess is somewhere . . . out there." Sam gestured to the open sea to the west.

"Out there? What's out there?"

Sam looked at the flat shimmering expanse of brilliant blue and green, stretching as far as the eye could see, as if the earth was a mammoth stretch of jewel-like brilliance, flat, endless.

"There? Nothing. Oh, if you headed south you would eventually hit New Guinea. But it's a big ocean, filled with a thousand islands we know and probably a thousand more chunks of rock we don't."

"So you're saying we might be on a wild-goose chase?"

"All I'm saying is . . . I don't know what's out there, and I doubt Rosa does. In fact—"

Tommy gave Sam a nudge. Sam turned back to the ship and saw Rosa and Bakali walking toward them.

"Wish I kept that cigarette," Tommy said. "I think we're about to find out where we're heading."

"I wanted to tell you what I am doing," said the captain.

Rosa and Bakali stood so that they blocked the early-morning sun. They looked like two dark shapes, ominous hulks.

"Great. I guessed we wouldn't stay here," Sam replied.

"Here?" Bakali said, talking through clenched teeth, tight on his cigar. Sam noticed that the stogie wasn't often lit, that Bakali, for all his swagger, nursed the cigar for most of the day. "Here—there is nothing."

"I noticed. So, Captain, where we headed?"

"Further out. We follow the island shelves, the great reefs. Tell me, what do you know about oysters?"

Sam looked at Tommy and grinned. "Not much."

Rosa moved to the side, and a brilliant slice of sunlight hit Sam square on the face.

"Sure you can find them on sandy bottoms protected by reefs, but you can also find the big ones deep, eighty meters deep. They like it where water's moving, currents from all over, come together."

"They like that?"

"Yes. And if there is freshwater current, off an island . . . then you get nice big oysters."

"And the big pearls," Bakali said.

"Good to know."

"Yes. So we move out there, looking, hunting. We may be out for longer time than I told you. So . . . I make sure. That okay for you?"

Sam nodded. "No plans to be anywhere else, Captain. So I guess this is as good a place as any."

"Me too," Tommy added quickly. But Sam could see that they weren't exactly waiting for Tommy's answer. They'd probably just as easily throw the kid over the side as chum for the fishing lines the ship trailed . . . to supplement the chef's store of food.

Rosa slapped Sam's back.

"Good. Then we keep going. To the unknown, eh? And maybe we get lucky, hm?"

Odd choice of words, Sam thought. *The unknown.*

Just didn't sound good.

Rosa and Bakali turned away, returning to Portuguese, talking about who knows what.

He turned to Tommy. "Hey kid. You want a smoke . . . *smoke.*"

Tommy grinned, and dug out a crumpled pack of cigarettes and lit up, the white smoke sailing up high to a nearly perfect blue sky.

27

The Indian Ocean

SAM DOZED BELOWDECKS, THE STEADY chug of the engines soothing in their repetitive rumbling.

Occasionally a crewman would enter the bunk area and make some noise and Sam would stir from his daytime sleep. A bit of a dream would remain, disconnected, part of some vision that vanished like cotton candy melting on his tongue.

For a moment he was a teenager back at St. Vinnie's when he first discovered a reason for going to Mass—to see the girls walking back from Communion, looking so sweet, so innocent.

So desirable.

Then another, reliving a battle between his older brother and his drunken father bellowing at each other, then finally shoving, until he saw his father thrown back into his chair, his cruel drunken rule finally over, defeated.

Then, being under water, the dives into the murky Sheepshead Bay harbor, dives where the yelling ended, the light faded, and there was peace, peace and—

Feeling—a little bite.

Some small pumpkin seed nipping his white tender skin.

Barely feeling it, but such a strange feeling when you know something wants to bite you, take a nibble—

So many incomplete dreams of home, dreams— maybe—of why he left and joined the Navy to begin with.

Dreams and nightmares that led here.

He turned over.

Someone shook his shoulder.

"Sam! Sam wake up."

Sam turned over. Tommy leaned over the bunk, still shaking him.

"I'm up, damn it. What the hell—"

"Sam, they see something."

Sam rubbed his eyes. In a moment he took in the dank bunks, the dim light from the exposed bulbs on the ceiling, the smell of salt and sweat.

"What?"

"You better come on deck."

The dreams, the images faded, and then gone as soon as Sam's feet hit the floor.

"What is it?"

Sam stood next to Rosa by the wheel.

"It's a pearl ship, see . . . one of the old ones. You can tell from the rigging, and small. But I see no one moving. We try radio, signal . . . nothing."

The words from this morning came back to Sam . . . *the unknown.*

"So what are you doing?" Sam realized that though Rosa was captain, he had slowly taken Sam into his confidence, treating him like the lieutenant that he was.

"We take a look. Maybe there is a problem. It's very strange."

Within minutes the *Mia Susana* was beside the ship. Sam left the wheelhouse and went starboard as Rosa brought his ship alongside and then threw the engines into reverse so that he rested a few meters away from the mystery ship.

It didn't take long for everyone to see what was going on aboard the other ship.

This close, the smell was overwhelming. The stench made Jorge gag, and some of the other crew brought their dirty hands up to their mouths to mask the foul odor.

Sam felt bile rise at the back of his throat. But he was more interested in what the hell happened here.

Tommy came and stood beside him.

"Sam, do you see that, over there?"

Tommy pointed aft on the small ship. At first Sam didn't see anything, then he made out what was clearly an arm extended out from behind some crates.

"Jesus," Sam said.

The ship drifted in the calm water, and Rosa had only to give the engine a little rev to keep the two ships close together.

"What is it, Sam?"

"Beats me kid. A painted ship on a painted ocean . . ."

"Hm?"

"A line from a poem. 'The Rime of the Ancient Mariner.' "

Then Rosa bellowed from the wheelhouse. "Ernesto? Come up here. Take the wheel."

From the sick look on the first mate's face, Sam guessed that he was glad to get away from the stench.

In moments, Rosa was at the railing. Most of the crew had backed up. Still fascinated, but wanting distance from the smell.

"We have to go aboard," Rosa said to no one in particular. "See what the hell happened. It's crazy. No one there."

"There's someone . . ." Sam said, pointing to the lifeless hand.

Rosa nodded. "So I go aboard."

"Me too," Sam said. Rosa turned and looked at Sam as if he might tell him no.

But instead he said, "Sure. You go too."

"I'll go," Bakali said.

Another nod from the captain. He turned back to the wheelhouse.

"Bring us closer, now!"

They waited while Ernesto had navigated the boat back and forth, edging closer to the ship. *It's good that the sea is so still,* Sam thought. *This could be a tricky maneuver.*

Then only a few feet separated the two boats.

"Now," Rosa said.

He climbed on top of the railing and jumped. Bakali followed, and then Sam pulled himself up and jumped.

And then they were on the ghost ship.

Sam coughed; the smell on board was like something getting stuck in your throat.

He walked over to the arm and discovered the first corpse.

The body was positioned as if the sailor had gone to sleep on the deck, curled up, arm stretched out. Now close up, Sam could see that what skin was left on the arm had dried brown and leathery, like parchment. The head had hair, and spots of leather skin, but also exposed sections of skull.

"What the hell . . . ?" Bakali said.

The swaggering Portuguese seemed rattled, and for the first time Sam saw him with some sympathy.

Sam shook his head.

He looked over at the *Susana*, now pulled away, probably to spare everyone from the stench.

"Maybe the answer's below," Sam said. And he took the lead, as the other two followed almost reluctantly.

The stench grew worse. It was unlike anything Sam had ever encountered, almost a living thing—if this ship wasn't obviously a place of death.

In a small mess, smaller even than the one on the *Susana*, two crewmen were hunched over a table. They looked as though they had drunk a lot of rum, and conked out sleeping but for the bony protrusions of skull, and the few skeletal fingers outstretched on the wooden table.

No more rum for these two.

"Sam, Bakali—here."

Sam followed the voice into a room, obviously the captain's quarters, still cramped, almost a closet . . . but some privacy.

Rosa stood there looking at the other captain.

The captain's shirt open, the exposed cavity of his chest on display.

In front of him . . . charts.

Rosa hesitated a moment, but then he came close, and turned the charts around.

"Shows where they were."

Bakali said some words in Portuguese, Rosa answered.

"What did you ask?"

"If there's anything there . . . about what happened."

Rosa shook his head. "*No* . . . nothing."

"Wait a minute," Bakali said.

He walked over to a small side table by the narrow bunk. A metal chest lay on the table, locked, as Bakali tried to pop the lid. Bakali took out his knife and started working the lock. "Maybe something in here . . ."

Sam wanted off this boat. He didn't know what killed everyone, but it looked like some disease, something poisonous. He noticed that the wood floor around the captain was dotted with dark maroon blotches. These people had been bleeding from open wounds, something killing them, making their bodies *ooze*.

Best to get the hell off here.

The chest popped open.

And inside, three white balls, shiny, glowing even in the gloom of this room. One nearly the size of a baseball, the others more like golf balls.

Bakali took one out.

"Mother of God . . . look at these."

Pearls. Giant, amazing . . . *pearls*.

Rosa walked over slowly.

And now Sam detected a shift in the two men. They had been focused on the mystery of this ship of death, but now that vanished as though some tropical gust had blown those concerns away.

And replaced it with something more basic.

How much were those pearls worth?

And then the thought, as yet unspoken, but Sam could guess what Rosa and Bakali were thinking.

Where did they come from, these incredible pearls? And were there more?

"Shut the chest," Rosa said. "We will bring it aboard and . . ."

He walked over to the captain's charts. Those too had drops of maroon on them.

"Not sure we should—"

Rosa's response was fast, almost violent. "Did you see them, those pearls? They came from—" He jabbed his finger on the chart showing where the ship had been. "—here. There could be more. We could be wealthy. *Rich!*"

Sam nodded. "Or dead. Like them. You don't know what—"

"It didn't come from diving, my Navy friend," Bakali said, swagger returning. "We have their charts, and we can find where they came from."

"And if we want to stay well, we best get off this ship now."

Bakali had the chest, Rosa the charts, and they started topside . . . and with a last look at the pathetic corpse of the captain, Sam followed them.

Ernesto tossed a wine bottle filled with gasoline onto the ship. The bottle smashed on the deck, and instantly flames spread over the ship. The dry wood and—Sam imagined—the dry bodies would probably immediately catch fire, burn quickly.

But were they burning the ship because of whatever diseases it might carry . . . or to preserve the secret of those pearls, a find like no other?

No one said anything as the ship drifted away now, completely aflame, the heat reaching Sam despite the distance.

Rosa turned the *Susana* away, then accelerated. . . .

After another minute, something on the burning ship exploded, sending fiery chunks of the deck flying into the sky.

In minutes, it was over, the sea quiet, the ship gone.

Behind them the sun had reached the sea, the sky above them darkening.

And Sam didn't say anything, certainly not to Tommy who brought him onto this ship, to this journey.

The thought: He wanted to get off, right here, right now.

But that, of course was impossible. . . .

28

Atlantic City, New Jersey

ANN SHUT THE DOOR TO the diving bell. She saw some of the people make a face as they slid in—the smell of sweat was overwhelming, and the few minutes of open door did little to dispel the hot, swamplike odor.

Must be what it's like in a jungle, Ann thought. *Sweating so much, and all the plants and trees closed in tight, so tight you almost can't breathe.*

She locked the door and went back to the controls for the bell.

Weeks after coming to the Steel Pier, she still was stuck putting people into the diving bell for the "adventure of a lifetime."

How much longer could she stand it? She wasn't sure.

She started her all-too-familiar spiel to the trapped tourists, now beginning to sink below the planks of the boardwalk. . . .

"You're about to travel . . ."

The bell sat on the bottom, while Ann looked at the clock. A few minutes for them to look out at nothing before she'd bring them up again.

"Having fun, kiddo?"

She turned around to see Johnny, Susan's boyfriend.

"Loads."

"You haven't showed up at the club on Fridays." He held his glance a few moments too long, and Ann looked away. A gorilla like this was the last thing she needed in her life. Right now, all she could think about was getting back to New York.

But money was still a problem.

"You know, a club like mine always does better when there are beautiful women in it. And you must know . . . you are some dish."

"Really? I haven't heard. Excuse me—"

She started to bring the diving bell up, accompanied with her script congratulating all the brave underwater explorers.

When it popped up, shimmering with the sea water cascading off it—a swim would be so great now—she pulled the door open. Johnny was still there.

"A dish like you could make some influential friends. You do want to stay here, right? You're a performer."

"So I thought."

The crowd in the bell emptied, giddy from their fast rise to the surface. Ann started to take tickets from the line of people waiting.

"Yeah, this is getting you nowhere fast. I suppose you heard by the way . . . the news from the Aquacade?"

The last person entered, and Ann shut the door, bolting them in.

"No? Turns out one of the girls showed up tipsy.

Nadler fired her. So now he's down one girl to dive with the horses. Heard you ride?"

Now she turned to him. The diving horses . . . at least that would be performing.

"I've done a lot of, you know, business dealings with Nadler. In fact, I do business with everyone along the whole damn boardwalk. I could put a word in for you."

"But he said if there was an opening—"

"Look, there are a lot of babes on the pier who can ride. Know what I'm saying?"

Ann realized that she was delaying the trip of the people locked in the bell. She put a hand up to Johnny, asking him to wait, and walked over to start the narrated journey.

When they were on the bottom, she walked back to him.

"You could put a word in for me? Get me the job?"

"Could do. But then, I'd like you to do something for me."

Ann rolled her eyes, but Johnny quickly laughed. "No, nothing like that, toots. All I want you to do is come to the club Friday. Have some fun. Be nice to the customers. Dance a little, drink a little. You do drink?"

"Not much."

"No matter. And that's it. So what do you say?"

How many more days could she go on running these crowds up and down in the diving bell, reading the same boring words, day in and day out?

She imagined the thrill of diving with horses. Sure, she didn't like the water, but she guessed she'd only be there for a few minutes, then out.

People would clap, cheer.

Almost like real showbiz.

"That's it, hm? That's all you want me to do?"

"That's it. Just come to the club."

"Deal," she said quickly.

Johnny grinned, and then stuck out his hand. He shook Ann's, enveloping her small hand in something that felt like a giant paw. Not someone she liked to get mad at her, she knew that for sure.

"There, that wasn't so hard, hm? Now I'll go find Nadler. See you around kiddo."

He turned and walked away from the diving bell.

Could he really do it, really get her the job . . . that easy?

Guess she'd find out soon enough.

Ann checked that there was nothing left behind in the bell after the last ride of the day. The sun had slipped below the taffy and game joints on the boardwalk, and the sky was darkening.

Maybe she had been stupid to believe Johnny.

Ann was stuck doing this until she had enough money to go back to New York, survive for a while, while she hunted for work.

If there was work to be found.

She saw a giant wad of still-wet gum under the circular metal bench. She pulled a small metal file that they gave her for just such a situation. She scraped the gum off the floor. It was still a bit wet, pliable.

Disgusting.

"Last time you'll have to do that, Ann."

Nadler stood in the doorway, and she stood up so fast that she nearly hit her head on the low roof.

"What?"

"I need a new rider for the diving horses. You did say you ride, right?"

A grin exploded on Ann's face. She nearly ran and gave Nadler a hug—before she was aware that she had the wad of gum on a metal file in her hand.

"Thank you. You won't regret it! I love horses, all animals. I'll work hard."

Nadler nodded. "Oh, it is hard work. We do six shows a day, seven on Saturday and Sunday. You'll be wet most of the day, Ann."

She thought then of the ocean, of her fear of the water. Could she really do this . . . forget that she'd be diving into the sea on a horse?

She'd have to. She wasn't about to let her fear stop her.

Nadler turned to walk away.

"Mr. Nadler, I was wondering—"

He stopped and turned back. "Yes?"

"Does it pay any more, I mean the diving horses. I was thinking—"

He laughed. "Of course it does. Not a fortune, Ann, but you are a performer. You may find that for the first time since you came here you have some pocket cash. Sound good?"

"Great. And thanks."

Nadler's eyes narrowed as if he was about to say something more . . . something serious.

A word of caution maybe? A warning?

But instead he just nodded. "You're welcome. See you at the paddock at the end of the pier, tomorrow, 7:30 AM sharp. One of the trainers will show you the ropes. And get a good night's sleep—you'll need it."

Nadler walked away, and despite his good advice, Ann doubted she'd get much sleep that night thinking about diving horses and the Atlantic Ocean.

29

On an uncharted island

THE GIRL RAN AS HARD as she could, scrambling to her
feet every time a root pulled her down. The jungle was
darker than anything she had ever seen, but even in
that darkness one could see the shapes of giant leaves
and the thick trunks of trees that towered unbelievably
high before completely covering the sky.

That, and the mammoth structures that blended
into the jungle, overgrown with trees and suffocating
vines. These monuments towered so high, dotted with
openings, all guarded by gigantic stone faces.

Looking up, the girl couldn't see any sky, no stars,
not any light at all from above.

But as she ran, the roars faded.

And where was she running?

She couldn't go back to the village, back to the wall.

No one who had been given to Kong ever returned.
They would not let her return. They would kill her.

She knew this.

And so, like some hunted animal, she kept racing
through the jungle and the night. She stopped in an
open area.

For some reason the bushes and plants were not so dense here. Now, for the first time, there was finally a piece of sky, an odd-shaped piece of dark black dotted with the small points of light.

She took a step, and the ground crunched beneath her feet in a strange way. She bent down and touched the ground, rough and crumbly under her fingers. She scooped some of the ground up and brought it to her nose.

She sniffed.

The burning smell made her yank her head back, the odor so much like the ground near the fires of the village, the strong smell of burnt wood.

Fire had been here, burning down trees, the giant plants . . . fire that opened up the sky, and made this an open place.

Open.

She was standing in the open, under the scant light—but light nonetheless.

Standing there, and so easily seen.

She started running again.

30

The Indian Ocean

"SO WHAT DO YOU THINK? The chief is a little loco, hm?"

Sam looked up at Bakali. "I don't know what to think. This is still all new to me, you know?"

"Oh, I do know. It shows, my friend. And that one—" He pointed to Tommy sitting in the bow as the boat plowed through the crystal-clear water, leaving a brilliant white wake as it steamed ahead. "That one could be dangerous. To you, to me, to any diver down with him."

"He's okay."

"Then you dive with him."

"Don't worry, I will. Tell me something. Ever do this before, go off on a hunt for a good pearl bed?"

"Like this? No. But then"—Bakali laughed—"never found a ship of dead men before, or pearls bigger than my *cojones*."

And even Sam had to laugh at that—though the images from the death ship, then the fire, seemed to be some line they had all crossed. A line crossing over to something now strange, deadly.

He didn't like it.

And there wasn't a damn thing he could do about it.

Bakali looked over the side. "Sure can see good down there. Be good when we dive."

But Sam had lifted his eyes to the horizon. Ahead— a line of clouds.

"Hey—see that? What's that you think?"

Bakali took the unlit cigar out of his mouth. "That? I don't know. Clouds?"

Sam looked at the low-lying clouds. They didn't go from one end of the horizon to the other, but instead seem centered at one spot.

"I don't know. Clouds go . . . up. These look like they're just hanging there. Hard to tell unless we get closer. But does look weird, no? Like a wall of fog rising from the sea."

"It will blow away. Things usually do out here. Except in typhoon season. Then, you know what? You might as well jump in the water with those weights around your neck and let them drag you right down to the bottom. Typhoons out here . . . they're killers."

"Hey! Hey everyone!"

Tommy yelled from the bow. "I just saw this big flying thing under the water, the size of car. God—what—"

Bakali answered. "Probably a manta ray. This is their kind of water. Not too deep, good reefs for lots of fishies for them to feed. Probably wasn't that big though." Then to Sam. "Kid gets excited, hm?"

Sam looked over the starboard side but didn't see anything.

But then the ship slowed. He and Bakali looked up to the wheelhouse.

The ship slowed . . . and then stopped.

Captain Rosa came out. "We drop anchor. Come on, everyone get moving."

And the crew, led by Ernesto, started hurrying to lower the ship's twin anchors.

Rosa came running down to Bakali and Sam.

"These are good waters to dive. Maybe sixty . . . seventy meters. No more. This could be a good place."

Sam stared at Rosa's eyes. *Gambler's eyes*, Sam guessed. *Used to following his hunches.*

"Should I suit up?" Bakali said.

But Rosa shook his head. "No. Help get the ship moored." He looked at Sam. "You, and your young friend. You go down first."

Sam stood up. This was a job, and Rosa was the boss.

"All right. I was wondering. You see that?"

He pointed at the fog bank.

Rosa gave it a cursory glance. "Not bad weather. Looks like fog."

"Ever see any fog like that before?"

Rosa gave it another look. "No. But this place here—it is barely on the charts. Maybe there is land there. Some land, usually some fog."

Sam looked at it. That might explain it. But the fog hadn't moved. In the beautiful, blue sky day, without a cloud in the sky, with a steady gentle wind from east. The clouds, the fog bank stayed in place.

A wind like that should do something . . . but the fog bank looked like it was painted onto the sky.

"We're going down?" Tommy said.

"Yes," Rosa answered. He patted Sam's shoulder. "You two. Maybe we get lucky here. When you see the big fish, sometimes the reefs are good, it's good eating for them."

One of the crewmen shouted something in Portuguese from the stern. Rosa nodded. "Okay—the stern is secure. Get into your suits. Go bring us some luck."

Sam looked at Tommy. Just one great adventure for him. And they walked over to the compressor, to the two tenders waiting to put their heavy dive outfits on them.

Tommy was ready ahead of Sam, so he moved to the metal platform first. His tender, a short grizzly man who spoke no English, fed him the tubes while Tommy clumsily stepped onto the platform and sat down on the heavy iron-mesh bench.

He gave a thumbs-up to the tender, who relayed the signal to the man working the winch. The platform started moving into the air, and then over the railing until it was suspended over the brilliant water.

Sam's tender carried his helmet to him and then started to place it over his head, fitting it snugly onto the places where it would be bolted.

The man worked quickly then, tightening the bolts corroded from years of brine and diving. When the wrench wouldn't move any more, he placed the lead horseshoe on Sam's shoulders. Forty pounds of dead-weight, and that—along with the boots and the weights at his midsection—would give him a speedy ride to the bottom.

The tender tapped Sam's faceplate.

Sam gave him a thumbs-up.

The metal platform had been brought back having disgorged Tommy, already rocketing to the bottom. Water streamed off the platform as they lowered it to the deck with a loud thud.

Sam stood up and walked to the platform, and sat down on the bench. Another thumbs-up to the tender, another relay, and the platform started up. Except this time it rose a bit wobbly, and Sam guessed he had plopped down off-center. He grabbed one of the trusses connected to a bar that ran along the top of the platform. He shifted his weight to the right.

That seemed to steady it. Sam leaned down and watched the platform sail over the railing. Then he could see the ocean below him, a bit less clear with the faceplate fogging up. That should clear once he hit the water . . . though he had had dives where the main faceplate had a perpetual foggy smear. Could ruin a dive. And that could easily add to the danger level. A bit of fog, and you missed stuff.

The platform lowered, until Sam sat waist deep in water.

It was time for him to step off and go down.

He checked his other gear; dive knife on his belt, a coupled of bags for pearls should they get lucky, or for oysters if they wanted to sample any beds they found. But if they were looking for where the giant pearls could be hiding, those oysters wouldn't fit in any bags.

Sam stood up. He checked that his air tubes and lifeline were free of the platform.

It all looked good. He stepped off the platform in the cumbersome suit and began his plunge to the bottom.

31

The Indian Ocean

THIRTY METERS, SAM THOUGHT.

Had to be closer to forty. Maybe more. And Rosa probably knew it. They couldn't stay down long at that depth.

And Sam had to wonder . . . did Bakali know how deep it was? Maybe that's why he wasn't in any hurry to dive.

Let *us* test the water, and the depth, first.

But when Sam tilted his head down, he finally saw the bottom.

And something more.

A mammoth reef that seemed to stretch in all directions. Though the color faded at this depth, the visibility was so good that Sam could still make out the rainbowlike shadings, from giant barrel-shaped coral to twisting branches of treelike coral that looked like some ancient bramble.

He looked for Tommy, and saw that he had already moved to a sandy area, a valley between two mountains of coral.

Tommy raised a hand to Sam and waved.

Sam looked down.

He was going to land on the fringe of one of the coral brambles. Not a great place to land, but there wasn't much he could do about it.

He braced his legs, and landed on a few of the twisted branches, crashing down a foot to stop his plunge.

He looked around for the best pathway to the sandy bottom and Tommy.

He started moving—a bit like mountain climbing. But now his suit, though still heavy enough to keep him down, wasn't so bulky that he couldn't move over the coral, using his boots to kick and hands to grab.

In minutes, he stood a few feet away from Tommy.

And he saw what he didn't see from atop the coral—the reason Tommy hadn't moved from the spot.

Sam took a giant stride off the last snarled mound of coral, snapping some of the beautiful arms in the process. But now he was on the flat sandy bottom.

Tommy's arm pointed straight ahead.

To a bed of oysters that seemed impossible.

Giant oysters—about a dozen or so, all different sizes, but they were all big, a few gigantic. Most were open, exposing the meat of the oysters siphoning the water as the current fed the shellfish. The largest ones were the size of a kitchen table, and none was smaller than a dinner plate.

"Wow," said Sam inside his helmet. Tommy couldn't

hear him, but for a moment Sam felt as though what he was looking at was so incredible as to be unreal.

Leading with his head, Sam came beside Tommy and patted his shoulder. He could see the kid's grin through the faceplate.

Then they both trudged closer to the mammoth oyster bed.

Amazing, Sam thought, now only feet away from the ring of giant oysters. He scanned the puffy meat inside, checking for any signs of pearls hidden within. He tapped Tommy and told him to check a few of the other open oysters farther down the bed.

But so far, they all appeared empty.

Could it be that these oysters, so giant, didn't produce pearls too easily?

A normal pearl would be lost in the slimy oyster flesh. *Might be worth digging around in one,* Sam thought, using his knife to cut through the meat.

The oyster would begin to close then—but his knife would quickly kill it, arresting the closing action.

Waste of a big animal, though he guessed the oyster wasn't much of an animal. No eyes, no arms, no hands. Even a snail had more personality.

Sam's personal joke made him grin.

For the moment his apprehension faded here. This was incredible and he was glad to be here—even if they didn't turn up any prize pearls.

He turned in Tommy's direction.

The other diver had knelt down, probably trying to get a good look inside the open oysters. They both had their lights on, but the water was so clear they really didn't need them. It could be that the yellow light might catch a bit of the shininess hidden beneath the oyster flesh.

Sam leaned close to the largest open oyster, his light now squarely falling onto its center.

Which is when he felt movement right behind him.

Tommy, he thought. *Maybe he found something.* Sam started to turn around.

It was difficult to turn in a dive suit. Sam knew that you had to be careful not to give yourself too much momentum, or all the deadweight that you carried could send you corkscrewing around, then tumbling to the ground.

Still, feeling something move behind you, something brush the back of your legs, was enough of a feeling to make Sam hurry to quickly see what was there.

He tried to use his hands to balance himself, almost dancerlike, as he twisted around.

He expected to see Tommy.

That's what he told himself.

Except some part of him knew it wasn't Tommy. Perhaps the fact that he felt the movement, felt something behind him, somewhere near his thighs, his knees.

So despite his reassuring thoughts, in that second he turned . . . *he knew it couldn't be Tommy.*

Sam's outstretched hands helped him keep his balance. But when he saw what was there he almost forgot about managing his deadweight momentum.

The crab was a species he had never seen before.

But that wasn't the thing that made him quickly take a step back. The crab was easily four feet long, and stood three feet high, even higher when it started to hold up its claws, mammoth pincers that rose another foot or two above its black marble eyes.

Eyes that looked right at him.

The crab waited, waving those pincers, twice the thickness of Sam's arm, even in this bulky suit. Waving them, and snapping them open and closed. The shell of the crab rose to a dome, bubbled with bony sharp outcrops like armor.

Sam had no doubt this thing could pull him apart with those pincers.

And though it was hard to read anything in those empty black eyes, eyes the size of an eight ball, Sam guessed that the crab's reluctance to move away meant that it viewed Sam as food.

His right hand slipped down to the knife at his belt.

It was time to quickly give the crab something to make it reconsider its course.

Bringing his knife up to a good striking angle so he could jam it at one of those damn eyes, or maybe right into the mouth that, now, he could see was lined with what looked like tiny snapping bits, almost like the claws.

But he would have to attack that without having those claws catch him. How strong were they? Could they get his arm, crunch down, and snap it in two?

He brought the knife to chest level, ready to plunge it forward, when something unexpected happened.

The crab *moved*. He imagined that it would lumber slowly forward, that he would have plenty of time to thrust his blade right into the thing.

But no. It moved fast.

What was the word? *Scuttled*.

Like the blue crabs they'd drag up from the traps in Brooklyn, dumped onto the dock, and then moving sideways with amazing speed as if each and every one of them knew that their life depended on how damn fast they moved away.

Except this one moved forward.

Like dueling, it came right at Sam with its arms flying like twin rapiers.

And it was so much more mobile than Sam. It moved effortlessly, with an even, jerky speed.

Sam stepped back, then again, when his left boot caught on something.

His right boot went back, lifted, and then lowered down to steady him. But the surface that his right boot landed on was uneven, curved.

Sam started to fall to one knee.

His right foot sat on an uneven surface. But worse, in stumbling, in trying to balance, he lost his knife.

He turned to see it spiraling, end over end, falling into the sand. He'd have to take a step to reach it. He had to retrieve it, because he guessed on the next parry from the crab, it would lock those giant claws on him.

Suddenly, there was this tremendous, horrible pressure surrounding his right leg.

He looked back, and saw what had happened.

He had stepped back, and then on *and* into the giant oyster. The oyster's reflex shut the giant bivalves on his leg. Shut tight, tighter until his leg was trapped. The pressure was painful, but not excruciating.

But he couldn't move his leg, couldn't get it out of the oyster, and most importantly, couldn't get his knife.

He looked up defenseless, now trapped, and saw the crab, only about a foot away, as its dull eyes still studied him ready for the next, and final, scuttle forward.

32

The Indian Ocean

THE CRAB SEEMED TO BE hesitating before attacking, as if such a trapped specimen must be too good to be true. Its twin antennae waved in the current, and the oversized claws were still held high. But it didn't move forward for the kill, at least not yet.

And Sam knew that the danger was not simply having those claws tear a chunk out of his leg. No, once they cut through his suit, the air pressure would drop, water could come in. If he couldn't maintain air pressure in his helmet, he might get a "squeeze" from the pressure drop; his face would get plastered against the faceplate like butter being smeared.

In seconds, he'd be dead.

The claws came down. Sam saw the angled legs of the crab dig into the sand.

And then . . .

From behind the crab, Tommy knelt down.

Sam had been so focused on the creature that he didn't even see Tommy move, didn't see him kneel *right* behind the crab, the knife held high, and then plunge it down.

Tommy had both hands on the knife.

The blade was an inch and a half wide and sharp, with a serrated edge at its pointed tip. A substantial knife. But would it be able to pierce the thick, bulbous shell of the crab?

The giant crab moved; it reared back and then began a jump right at Sam—at the same moment that Tommy's blade cut into the shell.

Sam almost expected the knife blade to bounce off, to slide away from the hard shell; or worse, break right off.

But the knife met no resistance.

Like a worm trying to avoid the inevitable hook, the crab twisted around, trying to get at whatever had hurt it. But Tommy had pulled the knife out quickly. He was kneeling and the crab could easily turn around and grab the kid's torso with both claws, cutting the other diver in two.

But Tommy rammed the knife down again hard, and then again, until the twisting crab, demented with pain, crazed with the fact of its death, turned to Tommy . . . but too late.

It stopped moving even as the trio of holes on the top of its bulbous shell erupted with a flow of fluid from inside. The fluid, its blood or whatever, looked purple in the water, swirling around Tommy, swirling now around Sam.

Then Sam was brought back to his real problem.

He was trapped by the giant shell, the pressure constant, his leg feeling numb below where the oyster kept trying to use its powerful muscle to close, to protect the living meat between the two shells.

Tommy stood up, and walked to the back of the shell.

Sam could see the kid's eyes, and a bit of a smile behind his faceplate.

Tommy had saved his life.

Sam could turn around and see what Tommy was doing.

The other diver hacked at the back of the oyster, at the seam where the two shells were held together.

And from the look of things, it wasn't easy work. Flakes of the muscle, or whatever the tendon was that held the shells together, peeled away as Tommy sliced at the seam. It was slow going, and already they had been down too long.

Sam looked ahead and saw the dead crab, now inanimate, the trio of holes on top of its shell nearly done shooting their spray into the sea.

Another look back at Tommy, and Sam could see that the blade was finally going deep—he was getting somewhere.

And then, Sam felt it. The terrible pressure on his leg began to relax. Not completely but enough so that the pain lessened, and he could again feel his lower leg.

Was his leg damaged? He wouldn't know that until he got out of the water.

Another look back, and now Tommy was jabbing the blade in, burying it completely inside the muscle, then sawing back and forth. And with each jab, with each series of saw motions, the hold on Sam's leg lessened . . .

Sam turned back to face the crab.

And something moved in front of him.

At first, he felt as if he hadn't really seen anything.

Just a blur, some iridescent grayish green blur, moving so fast. Like a burst of color flying by. Could have been a swirling current of some brilliant water, streaming by, rocketing by him.

Then Sam felt the force of that water, the wake from whatever had just gone by him.

And Sam knew that it was no current, no colorful underwater stream.

Something big had just passed.

He turned back to see if Tommy had noticed it. But the kid was lost to his cutting and sawing.

Instinctively, Sam decided to test whether he could pull his leg out of the oyster. As if something told him that it would be a good idea to test whether he could move, that moving right now might be a good thing.

Digging into the sand with his other leg, he began to slide out of the shell trap, the numbness making it seem like it was someone else's leg.

Out of the meat of the oyster, out of the lip, up over the lip of the two shells, then down to the sea floor, still numb, still a leg that belonged to someone else.

Reaching back, tapping Tommy.

No time to tell him thanks, to give him a smile, but to say—they had to get out of here now. They had to move.

He tapped Tommy's shoulder again, and pointed up.

But the kid was unaware that something else was going on here, that there was more than just the wonder of his great rescue of Sam. That something *new* was going on.

Sam thrust his arm straight up with as much force and urgency as he could.

Indicating . . . *Get the hell up now!*

But by then it was, of course, too late.

It came back. Only this time Sam could see the creature coming right at them from a distance.

There was no word, no image, no thing in Sam's mind or experience that would allow him to put a label on what he saw heading their way so quickly.

The head looked like a crocodile's; even from a distance, in this clear water, Sam easily saw the rows of teeth that lined both sides of the narrow V-shaped snout.

And that *head*, that jaw . . . it was easily as long as Sam. Which meant the thing itself had to be forty . . . fifty feet . . . or even more. As large as a bus.

And the rest of it looked fishlike, a tapered body, a massive cylinder with fins and flippers, all to help it move with amazing speed.

San started to turn and tell Tommy, warn him.

Thinking . . . how stupid of them not to know that all that crab blood would bring something.

Only in this case it brought something from hell.

Sometimes back at Sheepshead Bay the boats would get an occasional blue shark . . . five . . . six feet, but nasty-looking. And once, a great white, nearly ten feet, a monster, an eating machine that dwarfed its captors.

Toys compared with this thing. Minnows.

Tommy stood beside Sam, and finally the kid saw it. In just those few seconds remaining, Sam could imagine the horror ride Tommy's mind went on.

They were immobile, frozen. What could they do in just three, four seconds? Nothing.

Sam did start to reach down to his lifeline, to give it tugs to indicate *We have to come up!*

His gloved hand closed on his line. He looked at Tommy. And amazingly Tommy stared right at Sam as if neither of them could face looking forward, looking at the thing coming right at them.

It slid through the curling snakelike air hoses. Pushing them aside but not cutting them. There was enough slack so that the lines moved to either side.

Closer now, the jaws opened, and in that last moment, Sam could see bits of whitish meat hanging from the teeth, could see the dull purple inside its maw, could see its eyes, duller and darker than even the black eyes of those dead sharks.

Then—the maw wide open.

Sam tugged pathetically on his lifeline.

The crazed monster reptile finally there.

The maw *selecting* one of them.

Selecting Tommy.

Sam heard the jaws shut even as the trainlike bullet of a creature went flying into them.

The sound of all those teeth closing, locking shut.

And in that split second, Sam saw the upper torso of Tommy go rocketing away, the now-cut air hoses turning the two feet of helmeted head and torso into some kind of grotesque human balloon.

But Sam couldn't see anything else since the body of the sea creature now sent Sam flying to the side, cartwheeling, head over heels, his airflow suddenly stopped before landing on the sandy bottom.

He quickly tried to get his head up so he'd have breathable air in his helmet. He looked down at his suit. The skin of the thing had ripped it open in a dozen places, like small razors slicing through the tough material that resisted even the sharpest coral.

The hoses still worked.

And somehow he still had his lifeline in his hand.

Two sharp tugs.

Meaning *up, now!* Topside, they would know by now that one of the divers was in big trouble, the compressor struggling to send air into the open helmet.

Two tugs, but nothing happened.

How long would it take that creature to turn, to cut

around and start back for another bite, most likely opting for some fresh food?

Until . . . Sam felt himself rise.

So slowly, it was torture. But he couldn't come up fast, he'd get bent, be as good as dead.

A few feet above the bottom, and he saw Tommy's heavy boot, and two leg stumps, both looking like flares shooting out blood.

Maybe the blood will distract the thing, maybe it will go there, instead of shooting right to me.

And as Sam got hauled up, he realized that he was like a worm on a hook, dangling in the ocean, tempting the creature to have another giant bite.

He had to twist to see where it was. At first he couldn't see anything despite the water clarity. It was so hard to look back in the direction the sea creature went.

And he knew what it was by now. No legendary creature, no creature of myth. He had been to the museum as a kid, seen the array of bones showing ocean creatures that were air breathing, like crocodiles but monstrous . . . huge. It was something that had left the planet forever tens of millions of years ago.

And yet . . . here it was.

Twisting, turning until he saw a graying blur. Looking like a cloud, a mist in the water, until the blur began to pick up some definition.

It was coming back.

A look up at the surface.

A look . . . the surface still twenty feet away, the

pace slow, safe. So aware of the danger of rising quickly and having the nitrogen bubble into his veins.

It was a risk he had to take. Sam tugged the line again, two more times.

The message of urgency obvious.

They would react. But would they be in time?

33

Atlantic City, New Jersey

ANN STOOD BY THE PADDOCK, the horses still, the smell of hay and wood and leather comforting.

She looked at one mottled horse, with cowlike splotches over its back and hindquarters. Looked almost funny. She reached her hand up to the side of its head.

"Careful, miss—that one's been known to bite, he has."

But Ann's hand was already there, already stroking. Though the horse snorted, he gave no indication that he was about to nip at her.

"Seems calm to me."

The trainer, a short man named Eddy, with bandy legs, and mop of reddish curly hair, grinned. "He sure liked to take a bite at the last girl—but then she was someone who you might want to bite, if you know what I mean."

Ann grinned, still stroking the horse.

"Ann?"

Nadler came into the small paddock. "Good, you're here nice and early. Making friends with the ponies—

good for you. Look, this is Eddy's department, let him show you the ropes. You have any questions, let me know."

Hours before the show, Ann now would get a personal training session in the art of the diving horse. Though she could ride thanks to summers on her grandfather's farm while her mom toured, she wondered if this might be beyond her.

A horse . . . diving into the ocean.

Sounded ridiculous.

"I'll be fine," she said.

"Know you will. Take good care of her, Eddy. Got a feeling we'll be saying we knew her when, hm?"

Then Nadler left. The morning sun sliced through the open spaces of the back wall of the paddock. Strange that these horses lived their lives here, no fields to run through or graze in. Only the short trip to the Aquacade arena, a quick jump into the ocean. A dog paddle to a platform, and then back to wait for the next show.

Wouldn't blame a horse if it wanted to bite . . . or worse.

"This one, her name is Belle. Think someone thought it funny to call such a homely horse 'Belle.' "

"I don't think she's homely. She's cute, funny . . ."

"The kids do like her. More than the others."

Ann remembered the act she had been working on with Manny. Said he'd get them into a show soon. Baggy pants comedy, only *she* wore the pants. Goofy and funny, just like Belle.

"So, this the one you want to ride? You can have your pick."

Ann turned to him.

"Yes. I think we picked each other."

Belle neighed.

"Sure seems to like you. Okay . . . let's get her saddled up and ready to get wet. And you better get into your suit. Dressing room's—" Eddy pointed, a bit shy. "—that way."

Ann looked through a rack filled with pale green suits. She reached for one that looked small enough.

She checked that the door to the tiny dressing room was locked, and then slipped out of her skirt and blouse and pulled on the suit. Bathing caps sat on a rack above the line of suits.

One size fits all? she wondered. She picked one, and pulled it tight on top of her head. A fit, more or less.

She unlocked the door, and walked down the hallway that led to the paddock, then beyond to the arena.

Ann walked past the other horses, then down a corridor to an open area where Eddy stood with Belle, now saddled.

"Okay. Mr. Nadler says you've done a lot of riding, so I'll skip the basics. Because, there's a lot about this that isn't basic."

He gave the saddle a tug.

"This is extra tight so when you go flying through the air you shouldn't feel any movement. Guess the horses don't like it, but it will make you feel a whole lot better."

Ann could see that the cinch around the horse's flanks was tight. The horse's flesh bulged on either side.

That's probably why Belle bit people.

"The other thing . . . the first time you jump you will feel an urge to jump off the horse, to get free of it. *Don't*. Spooks the horse, and worse, you could find yourself landing under it. You hold on for dear life and smile as you do."

Show business. Well, Ann guessed it was better than some jobs she could have taken.

It wasn't the bottom, she told herself. *Or was it?*

"Okay, ready to give it try?"

Ann nodded.

"Okay, I'll walk Belle to the opening, you walk beside her."

Eddy grabbed the bridle and slowly led Belle to the opening.

"Now, just get on. Tight quarters, but you should have enough room."

Ann put a foot into the stirrups and pulled herself into a seated position on the saddle, and smoothly too, she thought.

Good—I didn't embarrass myself with that one.

"Great. Guess you do know your way around the ponies. Okay, when you hear the announcer introduce the act, then—"

"What will he say?"

"Hm?"

"The announcer—what will he say?"

"Oh, something like—" and Eddie raised his voice so that it filled the narrow confines of the paddock—"Ladies and gentlemen, get ready to see one of the world's most amazing feats, a beauty on a horse diving into the raging Atlantic Ocean . . . or something like that."

"Then I ride forward?"

"Hold on. Not so fast. Once through here, you come to a narrow walkway. It's tough for the horses, especially late in the day when it's gotten wet, and maybe slippery. You got to make sure that you go slowly, got it? The audience will wait. Builds suspense. At the top, you will turn and stop. That's when the announcer will say something else."

"Which will be?"

"Oh, you really do want to know the whole deal, hm. Something like . . . 'Ann Darrow riding the incredible Belle.' "

"Why not the incredible Ann Darrow riding Belle?"

"Cheeky? You can work out your introduction. After he says that, it's your show."

Even just hearing about this was exciting . . . especially the part that it was *her* show.

All eyes on her, waiting.

Pretty amazing, she thought.

"So, then, whenever you are ready, you bring Belle to the edge. Lean down close, and—well you'll have to trust this next one—give the horse a good strong kick with both heels."

"And that will do it?"

"Horse knows what to do. It will pull back a few feet, begin a gallop and run, jump, flying through the air."

"What's it like to hit the water?"

"Why have me spoil the fun for you now? You're going to experience it in a few minutes. Once you're in the ocean, the horse will swim as fast as it can to the platform that's lowered in the water. You're just along for the ride at that point. It will climb up, maybe shake off the water—so hold on tight—and then begin walking into that entrance over there. I can be there to take him if you want to take a bow."

Eddy flashed a grin.

"Most of the girls do."

Ann took a breath.

Not much scared her. But this? It sounded almost impossible. But they did it every day, five times a day, so it had to be possible, right?

"All set, Annie?"

She smiled at that. Sometimes Manny called her that, more of a long lost father than acting partner.

She nodded.

But she was anything but set.

34

CARL DENHAM WALKED INTO THE lobby of what was now the tallest building in the world—the Empire State Building.

He turned back to Preston. "Preston, will you get a load of this? Makes the Chrysler Building look like a dump."

From the gleaming stone floor, to the curves of the metal that lined the mammoth lobby, the building was impressive from the first glance.

"We have to go to the observation deck."

"Probably not open yet," Preston said. "I wonder why the backers wanted to meet so early."

Denham started walking again, to the bank of elevators to the side.

"I don't know—but let me do all the talking. I'm not exactly in the best bargaining position."

Denham pressed a button and an elevator opened as if it had been waiting for them. They got in, and he hit the button for the eighteenth floor.

"If it was me, I would have taken an office on the

highest floor. Kind of a waste to be here and not to be at the top."

The elevator stopped, and the doors slid open.

"Okay, let me work my magic . . ."

And he and Preston walked to the office.

While still listening, Denham tried to size up who was in the room. Maury Zelman he knew, and probably the one guy Denham had to please. The new people . . . Sid Nathanson, introduced as Zelman's assistant, and Tom Farragher, an "associate."

Associate? Farragher looked more like a button man for the mob. He didn't smile as he shook hands with Denham and Preston, and his eyes looked perpetually hooded and mean.

Not a customer to get mad at you.

Zelman looked at the other two men, and Denham guesses the time to talk "nice" was over.

"Denham, we lost a lot of money with your mess up north."

A body movement from Farragher, a shake of the head.

"But we know you're good."

"Sure," Denham said, "I can recover. I got a new script working, going to get some good location stuff as soon—"

Zelman held up his hand.

"That's just it, Denham. See, it's the damn location stuff that's so risky. Risky, costly, dangerous. You love it, but do audiences care? I mean, do they really care?"

"So what are you saying?"

Denham noticed Preston shift in his seat. Preston was Carl's most staunch defender, loved him, and loved his work. He hoped he remembered the warning to keep his trap shut.

"What we're saying is . . . lose the location stuff."

"For a jungle picture?"

"Sid, show him the layout."

The assistant ran to a table against the wall and scooped up a roll of architect's drawings.

Zelman stood up and unrolled the drawings on his desk.

"You see this place? Look, you got tons of room. You make your jungle or whatever the hell you want to right here. It's all yours."

Now Denham stood up.

"Make a jungle, with sets, in a studio? Where is this? And *what* is this?"

Preston stood up slowly, and came beside Carl.

"This, well, used to be a bakery, right Tom?"

The gangster look-alike nodded.

"We got it to settle some old debts. Gutted it. Made it a studio."

"You want me to make a jungle picture inside a *bakery? Me,* Carl Denham?"

"You can make a great jungle there, Carl. And just think how close this is."

"Oh really?"

"Just across the river, in Astoria."

"Queens. I'm going to shoot a jungle movie in Queens."

Zelman sat down. "Exactly."

Carl stood there looking at the open space. He was about to walk—there was no way he could do this. He gave Preston a quick side glance. Denham could read the cameraman's mind. *Let's blow this place.*

Kind of ruined Denham's taste for this building, this new wonder of the modern world. . . .

But then he nodded.

"Okay. Maybe I can do it. The stars will like it. And I can get any animals we need; you're right, it's a big damn space."

Now he felt Preston's eyes on him.

"Sure—it can be done. But—" Denham looked up. "You're going to have give me the budget, a reasonable budget to do it, to make the sets, get the animals, you know?"

"How much more reasonable?"

"Yeah. Maybe a fifteen percent increase."

Zelman looked out the window. He looked down at the streets, thinking—

"Ten percent. But that's it—there will be no more money."

"Okay. We got a deal." Denham stuck his hand out to Zelman, who took it without a great deal of enthusiasm. "And now, gentlemen, we better get going, we have a movie to make. Mind if I take these?" he asked, pointing to the plans.

"They're yours."

Denham scooped up the rolls, and started out of the office.

"And we will want to see footage soon, once you get your cast, get the show rolling."

"You got it," Denham said, as he pushed the inner office door open, and scurried out.

"Mind telling me why you agreed to that? You're going to make a film on sets?"

Walking down Broadway, Carl grabbed Preston's wrist.

"Don't you see what I did?"

"I see that you agreed to shoot a jungle movie in Queens."

"*And* I got more money. Money that is not going into sets. We'll do some shooting there. But I'll get my location stuff."

Preston stopped.

"How?"

"I run the budget, and I'll make sure some of that dough keeps Englehorn happy till we sail. Hell, by then I may have convinced Zelman that we need location stuff. At any rate, I'll get my location footage. It will still be a Carl Denham picture."

"And where is that location?"

Denham looked away.

"Good question. I want someplace new, someplace dangerous, exotic. Show people something they haven't seen before."

"And that is?"

"Dunno, Preston, my man. But I have a plan to find this place. A plan, and when I do—when I know where our secret location is—you will be the first to know. Now, how about some breakfast at Nedick's—talking money makes me nervous and hungry."

"Sure."

And Denham and Preston walked across the street, the morning sun now cutting through the Manhattan canyons as the busiest city in the world got ready to move into high speed on a hot July day.

35

Atlantic City, New Jersey

BELLE WALKED UP THE RAMP slowly, though Ann felt that the horse wanted to hurry. It had a lot of spirit, but she had to make sure the animal knew that Ann was in charge.

Its hooves made a loud clatter as it went step by careful step up . . . until Ann was higher than the rows of seats located at the end of the pier, higher, until Ann could see the sun sitting above the jewel-like glistening sea.

She felt a wind too, stronger up here.

It was beautiful—so much so that she missed it when the walkway turned, and came to an edge.

She had expected that there would be some barrier that she'd have to lift, something to pull, so the horse could then get to the edge and jump.

But instead, Belle turned, snorted . . . stamped one foot—right on the precipice.

"Okay girl, you know what to do. But it's my first time, so we're gonna take it nice and slow."

She looked down and saw Eddy by the edge of the Aquacade area.

He held his hands up to his mouth like a megaphone.
"Anytime you're ready, Ann."

Anytime I'm ready. . . .

Which is never.

She leaned down, holding the bridle close, leaning right into Belle's neck just as Eddy had instructed.

She got her feet positioned and ready for the kick.

"Okay, girl . . . show me how it's done."

She kicked the flanks of the animal as hard as she could. Couldn't feel good, and for a moment Belle reared her head back, and Ann had to hold on even harder.

But then the horse stepped back fast, and shot forward—until, before Ann knew it, she was flying through the air, then tilting down. And the ocean raced at her so fast that she was barely aware that they weren't on the platform anymore.

Then into the ocean—icy cold after feeling the morning heat up above.

But Belle knew what to do. And the horse surfaced, paddling to another ramp where it could climb up, then out of the water.

Ann blew some wet strands of hair away from her face, and saw Eddy, clapping.

"Well done, kiddo. Well done."

The horse climbed out, and Eddy was there with a treat, maybe a sugar cube Ann guessed.

"How was it?"

Ann was still holding on to the horse's neck for dear life.

"Terrifying."

"You did great. And Ann, you can let go now. This is where you get off the pony to the sound of thunderous applause."

She let go of the bridle, and stopped hugging the horse's neck.

"And when do I experience that?"

Eddy looked at his watch.

"Oh, in about two hours."

"Really?"

"Really. So go get dry, get some breakfast—you're part of the show now. And I'll make sure Belle is ready for you."

Just like Manny, she thought. Sweet, funny, and something so smart and good about this trainer.

Ann gave him a hug.

"Ow," Eddy said.

"Thanks for everything. Showing me what to do." Then she patted Belle. "And thank you too."

Belle raised her head and snorted.

And Ann very much doubted that the dappled horse would ever try to take a nip at her.

36

The Indian Ocean

SAM KELLY KEPT LOOKING DOWN at the red cloud of blood below him. He mentally kept counting out each second even as the *Susana* crew pulled him to the surface at the fastest possible speed, skirting the limit of a bends-free dive.

His helmet broke the surface, and through the cascading water he saw the hull of the boat, and then, he started quickly getting onto the metal platform, and was pulled up.

He started yelling at them even as they began unbolting his helmet.

But the tenders understood only Portuguese and his muffled yells only brought strange, worried expressions.

Until the helmet popped off.

"Get moving, get the hell out of here! Get your goddam anchors up now!"

Rosa stood there, shaking his head. "But Tommy, he is below, what hap—"

But then the sudden shouts of the tenders made Rosa turn around, and Sam watched them begin to pull in the air hoses, air hoses attached to now just a bloody severed head in a helmet. One of the tenders turned away and vomited on the deck of the ship.

"The kid's dead. Shit, something got him. Christ, get the anchors up," Sam said. "Now!"

"Dead? But how—"

"He's gone, and we will be too if you don't move *now*!"

Rosa turned away. "Bakali, Ernesto—hurry!"

Rosa yelled orders, and crewmen hurried fore and aft and started working on the anchor chains. Then—

"Ernesto, to the wheelhouse. Start the engines."

One of the dive tenders removed Sam's heavy horse collar.

"And tell him fast," Sam said quietly.

"Where, what direction?" Rosa asked.

"It doesn't the hell matter. Just away from here."

Rosa yelled again at his men at the anchors, obviously telling them to hurry. Sam knew that Rosa didn't have a clue what was wrong, what happened.

Which obviously said something for the power of the crazed and terrified look in Sam's eyes.

He heard more yells as the two anchors popped out of the water. The rumble of the engines picked up.

They started helping Sam out of his suit.

The creature broke the water only yards away.

In the daylight, with the blazing sun hitting the shimmering water, with all that light falling upon it, the creature looked as if there was no way it could be real.

For a moment, every person on that ship went perfectly still.

Sam saw that his estimate of its size was—if anything—low. It had to be closer to sixty feet. The sun made the twin rows of teeth glisten, stand out against the gray-green skin, pebbled by bumps and ridges.

"*Madre dio . . .*" Rosa whispered. Then: "Ernesto, move!"

And before the creature went below the water again, Sam saw that its tail, though still looking like a crocodile, was more tapered, more like some great fish tail, though this creature obviously breathed air.

It dived below the water.

The ship finally lurched forward.

Ernesto steered a course away from the spot they had been diving, back in the direction from where they came.

But Sam, now out of his dive suit, standing there, cold from the breeze or perhaps, he thought, the fear, had a thought that seemed so clear and obvious.

There was no *back*, there was no returning from this thing.

For a few moments, everyone stood quietly while the ship ran at its highest revs, the sea breeze in their faces, the hot Indian Ocean sunlight glimmering everywhere.

And each person, Sam knew, had to be praying—in whatever way they prayed, to whatever god ruled their life and nightmares.

Sam thought of his life, not a terribly long one so

far, his feeling that there had to be great adventures ahead, great discoveries—that the future had to be filled with unknown possibilities.

Then this other thought, new, feeling it for the first time—that his future might never come. All those possibilities suddenly gone, vanished into thin air.

He looked at everyone on deck, each locked into their own thoughts.

Sam wondered: *Is this the way we should be going . . . back?*

Or should we have gone farther, perhaps past the natural barrier of the reef and coral?

A good question.

As if in answer, something rammed the ship from the bottom, and sent it tilting to starboard.

The first blow from below the surface sent a wave of water cascading over the side. But then the second hit the stern of the boat, and now sent the bow dipping below the water. One of the crew went flying forward, but managed to grab the railing even as his legs went flying over the side.

The boat righted itself.

Rosa started yelling orders, and Sam stood there, arms locked on some fitting on the deck of the pearl ship, holding on for the next hit.

But Rosa's order had the ship turning, quickly coming around to the other direction, cutting into its own wake.

Then the course straightened.

Right for the fog bank.

Sam looked behind the boat, and he saw the creature rise again, its eyes giant black grapefruits watching the wooden prey race away, belching smoke and white foam.

It followed on the surface, its tail occasionally whipping the water behind it, but it didn't seem able to keep up with the boat.

It slipped under the water.

Sam turned back to the fog bank. What was Rosa doing? This wasn't the way back where they came from.

The boat steamed steady now, no more attacks from the creature. Sam ran up to the wheelhouse. He grabbed the handrails to the narrow ladder and climbed up.

"Captain Rosa, what are you doing?"

"Getting away from that thing. Is that . . . what attacked you?"

Sam nodded.

"What is it?" The captain's voice shook.

"I don't know." Sam gestured over his shoulder at the wall of fog. "Why there?"

"The ship, she's been hit . . . below the water line. We are taking water."

"You mean it's sinking?"

Rosa stopped to yell something to one of the crew below.

"Not sinking, but taking water. The pumps, they can keep it out for a while. But we have to fix it. We need some kind of shelter, no waves. And wood. And that, there. Behind that cloud, there's maybe land. Unknown land. But land with wood."

"So we're going there to fix the *Susana*?"

Rosa nodded. He looked right at Sam and asked again, though it wasn't a real question. "What the *hell* was it?"

Sam turned away. The fog bank loomed ahead, a wall of gray at the surface, close, closer, as they left the creature behind.

And Sam had to wonder, *Am I the only person on board wondering what's inside that bank of fog?*

Am I the only one who's worried?

On an uncharted island,
somewhere in the Indian Ocean

THE SOUND OF MOVEMENT, and the girl woke up.

Something outside.

Last night, she had found a fallen tree, its trunk split open. And the fallen tree made a covering over an indentation, a hollow in the dirt. Enough of an indentation to protect her, so the girl grunted and clawed and pulled herself into the hole.

Now she was fully awake. She sniffed, maybe smelling what had to be the droppings of the animals that also used this hole.

But now something was outside the tree trunk, walking around, stalking, perhaps wondering who was in its special hiding place. The space was so low that she had to twist her head to turn to look through the gap to the outside.

The girl saw legs—thin, green branchlike legs, thinner even than her arm. But they ended in a foot with three large curved claws, and each claw as long as one of her fingers. The claws dug into the ground as the legs moved.

She tilted her head some more, and she could see other legs, another pair, then craning up, still yet another pair of legs, and behind, even more legs.

There had to be six, maybe seven of the things outside. They pranced around as if impatient.

They knew she was there. Maybe they had smelled her.

Waiting.

Her breathing became shallow, as if she was trying to be very quiet.

Then she heard a loud *thwack*. Something began pecking, hammering at the wood above her. Then at another spot, the same sound echoed, then another.

Thwack . . . thwack . . . thwack . . .

The creatures stood on either side, and though she couldn't see them, what they were doing was clear.

Pecking, pounding the wood.

Their beaks chopping at the wood, like the birds high in the trees that worked the wood bark to get at the small insects.

Like that—only now these animals used their beaks, what must be their big hard bills, to hack at the wood above her.

She quickly turned left again, the grit of the dirt scratching her face.

Legs still there, still lifting up and now stamping the ground, claws curling in. So close she could have reached out and touched those clawed feet.

But then something else . . .

Creamy flakes of wood started flying, landing on the

ground, landing at the feet of these things. The flakes fell fast as the hacking above her kept up a constant rhythm.

Flakes falling, building into a pile outside her hole, her hiding place.

And worse, the sound above her, growing louder, clearer, as their hacking grew more insistent.

The girl covered her ears, the noise so loud now, so terrible in what it meant.

And the things outside seemed to know they were close too. They moved faster, changing position, their curved claws clutching at the ground, excited.

And what would happen once they were through?

That would be easy to imagine.

In a few moments they would have cut through the wooden roof. Their frenzy would grow, and they would begin the last few mad chops at the bark.

She started crying; death, so vicious and terrible, now so close.

Then—a new noise.

A thump, and the thunderous rumble of earth moving.

Her head still looked left, at her thin view of what was happening.

She saw the thin legs begin to *move,* but then a pair flew up—vanished!—only to be followed by the same pair of legs falling to the ground, now severed from whatever head and body it had.

Then another pair up, and another, only this time, one of the thin-legged creature's heads fell close to her viewing slit. She could see the bill, like a giant beak, but lined with razor-sharp teeth.

And she heard the new sounds—

When they were grabbed by whatever had come, the smaller creatures made a pitiful sound, a high-pitched squeal that hurt her ears.

The screeching of the creatures continued, even after their severed torsos fell to the ground.

Then . . .

Another foot. But this one . . . with massive claws as thick as some trees. She saw the gigantic foot step on one of the still-screeching things.

And then she saw the great head as it lowered, much too big for her to see all of it, leaning down, reaching down to eat one of the carcasses whole.

The monster stayed there, eating one body after the other, until all she could see outside now was the big creature. Nothing else was left; the area outside had all been picked clean.

And then the big feet stepped away; the log shook, the ground rumbling with the terrible thunder.

The animal roared, the sound so deep and long.

Then it took more steps away. All the other smaller creatures were dead; there was nothing left to eat outside the log.

So—it moved away.

It moved away.

But the girl herself didn't move again for a long time.

38

THE AUDIENCE LOOKED UP, shielding their eyes from the blazing sun. Ann was amazed that they could see her against so much brilliance.

But by now she knew how to time her act.

Bring Belle to the edge, wait until the announcer finished his spiel, then hesitate—

Ann herself felt the exciting tension, though after a bunch of dives it was starting to feel strangely normal.

She laughed at that. *Normal.* Diving from a platform into the ocean on a horse. If it wasn't true, people wouldn't believe it.

She leaned down and whispered close to Belle. "All set girl . . . let's fly."

She only had to give Belle the slightest kicks now—the horse knew to respond without a painful jolt.

And Ann guessed that if she treated Belle well . . . then the horse would treat her well too.

The kick, and Belle reared back.

In a second, Ann went flying through the air, holding on for dear life. The giant splash, a few breathless moments underwater, then surfacing to . . . applause.

It might not be Broadway. It might not even be burlesque. But with the people clapping, the kids wide-
eyed, and Belle paddling for dear life to get out of the
chilly sea, Ann had to admit that she loved this.

Ann opened the door to the apartment.

Her roommate popped out of the tiny bathroom.
"Ann, that you?"

"No, it's some crazy killer."

"We gave already," Susan said.

Ann walked into the small living room and fell into
the couch.

Then Susan walked out wearing a stylish short dress,
and—Ann thought—too much makeup. Cute and
sexy—but maybe *too* sexy.

"You're not sitting, are you?"

Ann looked left and right. If she couldn't perform
on a stage, then she'd just have to do her comedy material for them. She looked left and right.

"Why, it does appear that I *am* sitting. How very
observant."

Susan gave Ann's shoes a playful kick.

"Well, *unsit*. And get dolled up, kiddo. And change
these shoes."

"Why? I'm bushed. I still feel like I'm underwater.
Can't get my ears cleared. Thank God Belle doesn't
seem to like being under water eith—"

Ellie, the other roommate, came out, also dressed to
the nines.

"You going to a wedding too?"

"To Johnny's club. They have a band and a singer tonight. Maybe even someone funny. He said . . . *you* said you'd go."

Ann remembered her deal. He would put a word in with Nadler (and she could imagine how that was done) and she'd show up at the club, keeping their stock of young women full.

"Oh, not tonight. I really am—"

Susan sat on the frayed arm of the easy chair.

"He didn't say it like it was an option, toots. Said you agreed to come, and he'd like you there tonight." She looked up at Ellie, as if she might be speaking a language to Ann that she didn't understand.

"Think you gotta go, Ann," Ellie said.

"I gotta, hm?"

A deal's a deal, Ann thought. *Especially when it might not be too healthy to try to weasel out of it.*

"Okay." She stood up. "Give me ten to throw something on, get some makeup on my waterlogged face, and then we'll hit the club."

Susan gave her a big hug and laughed.

"You're going to love it!"

They sat at the same table, but there was no sign of Johnny. The big band played something that sounded like Glenn Miller, something new. Some people slow-danced, couples flirting . . . and Ann knew that this was another part of her life not exactly in great shape.

Was she ever going to meet a guy?

Would she ever fall in love? She was funny, but she

could also act. She wanted it all. And how did romance fit into any of that?

"How's your Manhattan?" Susan said, already a drink ahead of Ann.

"Great." Ann nursed the potent drink. She didn't imbibe regularly and something this strong could have her on the floor in no time.

She took a tiny sip.

Still, it would be nice to laugh. To flirt.

Some guy built with the dimensions of a door—boxy, with no neck—came over and asked Ellie to dance. Though Sally looked gorgeous, no one approached her.

Guess everyone knew better.

Then a short guy, with a bald dome of a head came over and asked Ann to dance.

She started to make an excuse." No, I'm just resting. Been a rough—"

"Why not enjoy yourself."

She turned around, and there was Johnny, standing behind Susan, his hands on her bare shoulders, near her neck. He smiled, but there was nothing friendly about his suggestion.

"You kids like this music. Go on. Mike here—he's a good guy, you know? A really good guy."

The only way out of this awkward moment seemed to be to accept the offer of a dance.

She turned to bald Mike, smiled, and stood up. "I'd be delighted," she said. He didn't seem to get the joke.

Out on the floor, it became a game of dodging

Mike's feet. His shoes seemed to be happy only when stepping on Ann. Fortunately, she got into a rhythm of avoiding them.

He did try to talk to her, and there was nothing he could do about that, even though she stood a good six inches taller.

"So, you know Johnny a long time?" he said.

"I don't know him at all. My roommate does."

"Oh, it just seemed like you were, you know, one of his people."

"Well—'you know'—I'm not."

The troll looked back at the table, where Johnny now sat with Susan, his arm around her, whispering, leaning into her, stealing kisses.

"He's a bit stressed tonight. Had a little problem with a run from Nova Scotia. Some other mug thought it was his booze. Happens all the time. But—I dunno—this might be something bigger."

Great, thought Ann. *Now I have to listen to the business dealings of Susan's gangster, as told by a dwarf.*

"Yeah, he seems a bit tense tonight."

Ann looked at Johnny and Susan, now openly kissing.

"He doesn't look that tense to me."

And then mercifully the song ended.

Ellie came back about the same time as Ann. Johnny surfaced. "I ordered you two dolls more drinks."

"I wasn't done with my first," Ann said.

Johnny laughed. "So now you got two drinks."

Ann let Ellie sit down next to Susan, keeping herself as far from the gangster as possible. He looked her in the eyes as if he had spotted her maneuver.

"You should loosen up. Have some fun. Susan always has fun here."

"I had a busy day."

Another laugh, "Oh yeah, jumping on those horses."

"*With*. We jump together."

"Still pretty wacky if you ask me, hm Susan? Diving horses. Sheesh, what people won't pay to see."

Ann was about to answer—something she could do in a heartbeat. She had dealt with enough Manhattan guys with their wisecracks and smirks.

But this was different. She turned to Ellie.

"I need the powder room, Ellie. Care to join me?"

Ellie nodded.

And Johnny said, "Don't be long. Might start to miss you." He quickly turned to Susan, "Just kidding, doll. Just a joke."

Ann and Ellie sailed to the powder room, past an opaque glass door to the side of the stage.

They were about to leave the restroom, when Ann grabbed Ellie's wrist.

"Look, I don't want to stay here much longer. That mug of Susan's keeps looking at me. Makes me want to throw my drink in his face."

Ellie's face instantly registered horror.

"Don't do that."

"No, I won't. But I need to leave. Maybe you can

say you're not well. I could go with you. He wouldn't believe me."

"No, he wouldn't."

"So, deal?"

Ellie nodded. "Deal."

Ann opened the door.

The music had turned more up-tempo, and the dance floor filled, the horns so loud, the bandleader singing.

But then Ann heard something else.

Something outside . . . the screech of tires. Just audible over the sound of the band.

Ellie started for the table.

"Wait," Ann said.

She always had good instincts; that's what her mother said. Used to tell her that they could be real useful if she ever got to work in the theater.

Good instincts . . .

Screeching tires.

"What is it?" Ellie said.

Ann started to answer.

"Don't you—"

But then from the side, and the rear, all the doors of the club opened.

Not just opened, *flew* open, as if kicked, rammed open.

Through the open doors, a small army of men in black suits, hats pulled low—just like the movies.

And just like the movies, they all carried guns.

39

The Indian Ocean

THE *MIA SUSANA* CHUGGED STRAIGHT at the fog bank. One crewman—younger than Tommy—sat at the bow, checking the water depth, looking out for any sign of coral outcrops clawing to the surface.

Younger than Tommy . . . A kid. With his goofy smile, his life ahead of him. *And I probably owe my life to him,* Sam thought.

Probably?

No, I do *owe my life to Tommy.*

Then killed so brutally. Was Tommy the canary?

Sam's dad used to talk about working the mines when he first came to the States, something newcomers drifted into. A trap, if they didn't do something to escape the deadly work belowground.

And he told Sam about the canary. How they went down with a sweet yellow bird in a cage. Sometimes it sang in the caverns below, filling the gloomy shafts with a strange, beautiful sound.

But if the canary keeled over, if the canary died, all the miners began a mad scramble out of the shaft, away from the invisible killer that claimed the canary first, away from the poisonous gas.

Now, with Tommy gone, Sam thought of the kid like that, like a canary. Only instead of scrambling away, now they headed deeper into the unknown.

He looked down the side. The water seemed to darken the closer they got to the fog bank, losing the lustrous blue-green clarity it had only a hundred meters or so back.

Now the sky it turned gray—still clear enough to see, but losing color, like puffy white clouds turning into the dark thunderheads, ready to unleash thunder, lightning, and sheets of rain.

Someone emerged from the cramped belowdecks and yelled at Rosa.

Probably a report on the pumps. The ship was taking on water after being rammed, and the pumps worked to keep the water out.

When Sam questioned this move—looking for landfall—Rosa made it clear why he was worried.

"The pumps, they are old. They work, maybe twenty . . . twenty-four hours. If we are lucky. But then, they will stop. Need gears fixed, parts oiled. And when that happens, this ship will sink."

He looked Sam right in the eye.

He didn't need to say what that would mean. Even if there wasn't some kind of monster creature in the water, there were plenty of other more familiar things that would be interested in the floating, bobbing bodies.

Plenty.

Tommy's death could only . . . be a beginning.

Sam looked up. The fog bank ahead now reached to the zenith.

This is crazy, Sam thought. Steaming here. Rosa's instincts told him that the low-lying fog meant land, plants, animals—

In a few minutes they'd know.

Sam gripped the railing of the ship. He wished he still believed in God the way he was brought up to in St. Vinnie's. But those days were long gone. Hands tight on the rail, Sam took a breath as the ship sailed into the fog.

The fog engulfed the boat. Suddenly even the deck itself, with the massive compressors, the wheelhouse, turned blurry, even vanishing for a moment. The crewman looking at the sea could no longer tell anything about the depth. He ran for a line to drop to check the depth.

We could easily wreck the goddamn ship here, Sam thought.

The engine slowed, so now it barely glided through the dense smoky cloud.

Living in San Francisco, Sam had experienced plenty of fog. But this was different—it immediately made his skin wet, and when he rubbed his bare arms, they felt slick, almost slimy.

And the *smell*—full of strong odors that he couldn't place at all. The closest . . . one day when he went to the botanical gardens on a chilly rainy day, and in one warm hothouse, he sniffed the odors given off by the plants, the vines, the dirt, the sod. Such a primal stench.

It was like that, but incredibly stronger.

Another shout from below, monitoring the pumps. Rosa called out to the crewman sitting on the bow. Sam saw him shrug, and then shout something back.

"*No*, Captain . . ."

He couldn't see anything. They were steaming blind save for the line.

And the fact that the ship moved so slowly made the suspense that much more prolonged, that much more unbearable, until finally, amazingly . . . the fog began to thin.

It thinned, like layers of a plant being peeled back, and the wetness went away, the darkness of the fog lightened to something filmy, and then finally they were through it.

They had passed the fog bank.

Sam took a sniff. The smell was still there; if anything, it was stronger.

And ahead—land.

Rosa worked the boat back and forth, nudging closer to a rocky coast that led up to what seemed like a difficult climb and a ledge.

"Why not look for a beach?" Sam said. It seemed to him this wasn't the ideal spot to try to go ashore.

Rosa shook his head.

"How long have you sailed these waters?"

"I've never sailed these waters. It just seems to me—"

Rosa spit out the side window of the wheelhouse. The old salt was scared. That's one thing Sam could tell.

"Then you don't *know* about these islands. This place, this island is on no chart. Who knows who has come here before, and never come back. Who knows who is living here!" He fixed Sam with his watery, rheumy eyes, crisscrossed with red veins.

"What do you mean?"

"We go to a beach, we find people here maybe. They find us. Anything could happen."

"You're talking cannibals?" Sam laughed.

But Rosa didn't.

"There's a reason this island is on no chart—*no* chart! A reason. I don't want to find out what it is."

Sam looked at the coast; a massive jumble of rocks led to a rocky slope filled with more oversized boulders . . . as though a giant angry kid had tossed them down from the ledge above.

And the ledge—Sam had never seen such a sight before, as though someone had hacked away a piece of a mountain, leaving a sheer cliff.

For a minute, staring at it, nobody said anything.

Had anyone ever seen anything like this . . . ?

"Going to be damn hard to get wood down from there."

"We will just toss it—into the sea." Rosa stuck his head out and yelled to Ernesto. "Drop anchors!"

They sat twenty meters off the shore, in a protected curve of land, surrounded by massive boulders as the churning sea sent up spits of foamy water on all sides. After they found wood on the island, they'd cut it to make repairs, at least enough to get the boat to Sumatra.

That was the plan.

The anchors fell from the bow and stern. Rosa cut the engines, and now Sam only heard the rumble of the pump engine below, the ticking bomb.

The captain put a hand on Sam's shoulder.

"You—you will go ashore with us?"

"You're going?" Sam said.

Rosa nodded. Sam thought a moment, each step in this journey feeling ever more like a trap, more like the giant shell that closed on his leg.

"Sure."

Rosa managed a small smile.

"Good, then. Let's go."

They left the wheelhouse for the small dinghy that would take them ashore.

40

On an uncharted island,
somewhere in the Indian Ocean

ONE CREWMAN STAYED WITH THE rowboat, whose narrow planks would be of no use repairing the gash in the hull.

Another stayed with the ship and the pump. The others, including Jorge, Ernesto, and three other crewmen followed Rosa up the rocky slope to the cliff edge.

There were three guns on board.

Ernesto had one—"This is my own," he announced with pride.

Rosa had one, a small .45 caliber that he stuck in his pocket. The other, a matching .45, he handed to Sam. Then Rosa handed each a handful of shells.

Not much of a match if they did run into cannibals.

Cannibals . . . the idea seemed ridiculous.

But he kept coming back to Rosa's point. This island was, admittedly, off the shipping lanes. Still—to be undiscovered, to have a big blank spot on the charts, did raise the question: *Had people come here? Had something happened?*

The three crewmen, looking not at all happy, carried

saws and rope. The plan was to find a tree that could provide enough hardwood to repair the hull. Sam imagined he might have to go under again to do some work from beneath the boat.

Not something he looked forward to.

He kept replaying what happened, the images of Tommy before the attack, then the helmet, his head gushing, legs pumping blood into the water. And as bad—almost sick—as Sam felt about the kid, he could remember even more vivdly his own fear, his own prayer to God that he didn't believe it . . .

Let me get out of this alive . . .

He grabbed a sharp-edged slab of rock, and pulled himself on top of it, less climbing than crawling onto the slab that sat at an odd angle.

That's what he wanted. To get out of this alive. And he didn't let himself think of what the chances of that occurring could really be.

Sam reached down and gave Rosa a hand getting up to the cliff edge. The other crew stood there, unsure where to go and what to do.

And he didn't blame them. He had expected a jungle of some kind up here, but the towering plants and the twisting vines that curled around the massive trees were unlike anything Sam had ever seen, even larger than the redwoods.

Rosa stood up, and now he too looked.

"Ever see anything like this, Captain?"

Rosa shook his head. "No, everything is so much

bigger, and look—that tree there. What is it? Look at the leaves."

Sam nodded, and looked around. The whole setting—*gargantuan* is a word that came to mind—had the crew rattled.

Then Sam saw something else, nearly covered with the vines, shielded by the massive trees. At first they looked like natural formations, giant stone pillars that somehow ended up next to what had to be a volcanic mountain.

But as Sam looked he could see . . . they weren't pillars. They weren't just random piles of stone next to the mountain.

They were sculpted.

What looked like eyes, hooded and weathered with age, and a sloping brow, reminded him of pictures copied from the tombs of the pharaohs. Like that—but so different at the same time.

Something . . . some *people* had been here. Made them—and now—

They were gone?

He watched Rosa look left and right, not having noticed the statues hidden by the jungle.

"None of these trees will work. They are all too big. Take us days to cut one down, to make planks."

The captain rubbed his chin.

"We have to go deeper into the jungle, find some smaller trees, something we can cut."

But Bakali came beside him. "Captain, you yourself said no one knows about this island. Maybe it's not a good idea, going deeper into this jungle? We don't know what's there."

"He's got a point," Sam added. He pointed into the jungle, to the stone mammoth sculptures. "See them?"

Rosa stopped and looked.

Then a single word, filled with resignation, almost hopeless. "Yes."

"Maybe we aren't alone here."

But then Rosa turned back to Sam. "And what are we supposed to do? Run the ship until the pumps give out? Let her sink? Want to take your chances in the water. With that . . . monster, whatever it was? You've seen the sharks. Is that what you want to do?"

"Yeah," Sam said. "Right. We have no choice. Despite the statues . . . despite whoever the hell might be here."

Bakali was quiet as Rosa barked some orders to the other crew, and then took the first step into the dense wall of the darkest green that Sam ever saw.

They navigated slowly through the jungle, in between the towering trees, and the rest of the crew looked at the strange sculptures as they walked by. Not close enough to touch them, but close enough to make out clearly now the shape of heads, elongated, exaggerated. Could that have been the result of weathering over . . . centuries . . . or more?

Were these gods? Or did the people on the island look like that? And were they still here?

They pressed on.

Even if they each were equipped with machetes, this would be a tough trek. The tallest trees grew close together, standing abreast, and any open space was filled with the twisting vines thicker than the air hoses.

And the ferns . . . .

They had to be ferns, Sam told himself. But ten, twenty feet tall, with spores under their leaves the size of a half dollar.

There was one good thing, he told himself.

No animals.

Because if the plants were this large, the trees—

God, what were the animals like?

Then Rosa shouted, calling back to the line of men. "Ahead—look!—it opens up. We find something there."

And Sam could see a bit of sky, and the mountain to the right that rose nearly straight up alongside this chunk of the jungle. And he thought: *Let's cut our damn tree and get the hell out of here.*

How long had the girl been running?

Once it turned light, she started running again, always whipping her head from side to side, checking that nothing had spotted her, that nothing had decided to hunt her.

In the light of day, she passed a circle of stones, all carved with twisting shapes and figures, some showing grim faces that looked down at her, unblinking.

And once she nearly stumbled onto a herd of things, animals with small heads and gigantic curved bodies.

Smaller ones traveled beside them, babies with mothers.

She froze then—barely breathing—waiting until the herd moved on.

Then running again, racing over the same place just traveled by the herd, stepping into steaming piles of their droppings.

Across the path of the herd, she moved faster now, past the jagged mountain to her left.

But then—

She stopped—as soon as she heard the voices.

The words were strange, without meaning to her.

She stopped, and then she saw the men, coming through a thick cluster of trees, to an opening, near the mountain.

She took a step backward. Onto a twisted root, dry and brittle.

It *snapped* with a clear sound that carried over the opening.

One of the men looked at her.

The girl turned around, back the way she came.

But she soon saw that now . . . *now* that was no longer a way she could run.

41

Atlantic City, New Jersey

ELLIE BACKED UP, AND TRIED to pull Ann with her.

The gunmen at the doors started firing, and in a second the club filled with blue smoke that made the scene dreamlike. The patrons scrambled to the floor; it didn't look like the gunmen were targeting anyone. But their guns blew holes in the walls and the tables, the sound of bullets mixing with the deafening screaming.

Then the people started running, while others ducked under tables.

Looks like Johnny got someone mad.

"Susan," Ann whispered.

She saw Johnny crawling on the floor, no big-time mob boss now, and right behind him, on all fours, the short bald guy, and other hoods.

But she could also see Susan on the floor, under the tables, motionless.

Frozen.

"Susan's not moving," Ann said. She looked around the room.

"What are you going to do?"

Ann turned to Ellie. "She's not moving—I'm going to get her."

Ellie's eyes widened. "You do know they're firing real bullets."

"Yeah, but looks like all they want to do is destroy the club . . . which they've done a pretty good job of . . ."

The gunfire took on a rhythm as the men at the doors fired, shooting more walls, the stage, the deserted tables, the blue smoke like a fog hanging over the room.

And then Ann bolted across the dance floor, through the cloud of acrid smoke.

She ran to one of the tables on the left, and then crouched down, scrambling on her hands and knees to Susan, who had her hands locked over her ears, crying—her mascaraed eyes turned into black clownlike pools.

"Come on. You got to move."

Susan shook her head. She wasn't going anywhere.

There was no time for argument. Ann grabbed her right wrist, then turned back to the line of tables leading to a side exit.

She tugged hard, and Susan could have stopped them both if she decided that she wanted to be a deadweight.

But like pulling a kid out from under a bed, telling him that there are no monsters in the room, that it's safe . . . Ann kept moving, and Susan followed.

*   *   *

The gunmen turned and started to leave.

A last burst of fire, then quiet.

Ann looked up and saw a side door, now open, the warm summer air letting some of the smoke escape.

She turned back to Susan.

"Now we run. Got it?"

Mute, Susan nodded.

Ann stood up, and pulled Susan with her, also standing, running. She didn't dare look back. Who knew whether the gunmen would change their minds and start shooting people.

Running outside, seeing cars screaming away from the roadside speakeasy, people still crying, screaming.

Ellie came up to them.

"Come on. The police will be here in minutes. We got to leave now."

Ann nodded, and heard the first distant siren.

But before they started walking away from the club, Susan grabbed Ann's hand.

"Thank you. You saved me."

Ann laughed. "Isn't that what we're here for? To save each other. Maybe someday, I'll need some saving."

Susan gave her a hug, hard, tight, squeezing.

Then the three women started moving quickly away from the smoky debris-filled room that used to be a nightclub.

42

On an uncharted island

SAM HEARD THE SOUND, TURNED, and then saw a pair of eyes looking right at him.

He reached out and grabbed Rosa.

"Look!"

In the shadow of the mountain that rose close beside him, the strange-looking girl with tan skin and wide, terrified eyes nearly blended into the plants that circled this open area.

Sam had only a few seconds to look at her eyes, gleaming like a cat's eyes in the leafy shadows. He might have expected someone who looked like some South Seas islander. But her look was indefinable, with her straight brown hair and dark eyes. Sam watched her turn and start to head back into the depths of the jungle.

"Wait! Stop!" he yelled.

She was running full out back into the jungle, back to a place where they'd never find her. Except, as Sam started across the open area, he saw her stop. Then he saw why.

* * *

Towering above the ferns and trees, the creature took lumbering steps right at the girl.

Its giant eyes sparkled in the light as it used its ridiculously small arms to push away the entangling vines, and plants.

Like every New York kid, Sam had been led to the Museum of Natural History, spent long minutes staring up at the bony giant head, the inches-long teeth of what they called . . . a *Tyrannosaurus rex*.

King of the dinosaurs.

This was like that. Only bigger.

Bigger than any T. rex, a vast mountain of a lizard . . .

Call it a V. rex, Sam thought, *that is, if anyone ever gets around to naming the damn thing.*

Sam's body immediately went cold; a wave of icy water crashing over him. A land dinosaur, alive, just like the monster that took Tommy, monsters, prehistoric things that should have vanished tens of millions of years ago. Here, living on this island.

The girl stood frozen. The *V. rex* moved quickly. A few steps and it would be able to scoop her up in the mammoth head of teeth.

All this—in seconds.

Then Sam started running toward the girl, toward the dinosaur, while the men behind him started screaming.

Sam locked his hands onto the girl's bare shoulders.

She didn't turn to face him. And for a moment, Sam

thought that the girl would remain fixed to the ground with the dinosaur only two, maybe three steps away from her.

But then she turned back to Sam. Her young face cut and scratched, dotted with mud.

Sam started pulling her along back to the opening.

He heard—and felt—one of the giant feet land behind them, feeling not only the ground shudder but the wind made by the movement.

There's no way we can outrun it.

But then the jungle—the dark and overgrown jungle—came to their aide.

The *V. rex* had to navigate past a tree in its way. Sam now risked a quick glance back to see the creature dumbly push against the tree. And then when the tree didn't go down easily, the *V. rex* leaned down with an amazing smooth motion, and started cutting a path around it.

That bought them a few precious seconds.

When Sam reached the clearing, the men had backed up against the sheer mountain face. There was no going anywhere, not on this slab of rock that led directly up.

And no way to head back to the cliff edge. Too far to go, too much time for the dinosaur to catch them.

The creature bellowed, now at the clearing.

Sam looked around. Rosa and Bakali both had their guns out. Pea shooters against this thing.

He looked along the mountain's edge, searching for something, anything that might protect them.

And there—a few hundred yards away, he saw an opening; no telling how big it could be. No telling if they could make it.

He started pulling the girl toward the opening, yelling to the others at the same time as the *V. rex* roared . . . "If you want to stay alive—*run!*"

Sam turned back—an action primitive and irresistible. He had to know whether survival was still a possibility.

When he turned, he saw the line of men behind him, all running as fast as they could. But the dinosaur had reached the mountain opening and now moved, unobstructed.

And just as Sam looked, he saw the dinosaur lean down, in an almost snakelike move, and bite down on the last in the line, an old crewman who—as luck would have it—could not run as fast as the others.

The *V. rex* threw its head back, jaws open wide, so unbelievably wide, as it engulfed the crewman so only his legs stuck out.

Sam snapped forward. Twenty yards—*they might make it,* then—if only it did provide some cover.

Another look. The dinosaur biting down, then using its massive tongue to pull in the bloody, dangling legs. An amazing eating machine. And all the time it did that, it didn't slow in its race to catch them.

Clawed feet pounding forward, jaws chewing, swallowing, a devouring locomotive from the past still racing toward them.

They reached the opening—only about four feet high, a dark hole into the mountain wall.

"Just run in," he said to the girl, even though he imagined that she didn't understand.

But he was wrong there.

She did understand, darting fast, actually pulling away from Sam, into the hole, this cave with its narrow opening.

Now Sam followed her, running inside.

He had one thought as he threw himself into the hole. What if it isn't a cave? What if it is some thin depression, no more than a few feet deep, and then we're all bunched up on the inside, exposed, easy pickings for the creature?

The carnage would be quick, total.

It wouldn't last long, that's one good thing, Sam thought. They'd be dead, eaten—fast.

Sam rolled into the hole as if sliding into home plate at the Marine Park baseball field—when nothing mattered than beating the ball to the catcher.

Rolled, and kept rolling. He landed on the girl, and instinctively she wrapped her arms around him, and held on tight.

Then the others jumped into the cave: Rosa, Bakali, Ernesto, Jorge, another crewman—all safely getting into the cave.

Without saying a word, everyone started scrambling on their bottoms far away from that opening, even though Sam could tell that it was much too small for the dinosaur.

The girl still held on to him as he scuttled back.

Sam hit a rock and stopped.

All eyes were on their small odd-shaped window to the light outside. They sat—and waited.

BOOK THREE
Destiny

43

Somewhere above the Atlantic Ocean

DR. LEONARD MLODINOW LEANED CLOSE to the angled window and looked down at the sea below.

How high were they now? Last night, the zeppelin had hit some stormy weather, and Mlodinow felt it climb at an angle to get out of the weather.

But it didn't work—and the zeppelin sailed through the rough weather as though it kept hitting rocks on a dirt road.

And Mlodinow's biggest fear wasn't that something would happen to him.

No. His fear was for what the *Graf Zeppelin* carried in its cargo hold, what he was bringing to New York City. Even now when he thought about it, it gave him a giddy feeling of both excitement . . . and fear.

Excitement because it was the most extraordinary thing that had ever happened to him as a paleontologist. New discoveries happened all the time in the field. Roy Chapman Andrews leading landmark expeditions to the Gobi, making amazing discoveries . . . All very thrilling.

But this? It made everything else take a sleepy second place.

Then—the *fear*.

Here he had to admit to himself that he hadn't quite thought through all the implications. And that was quite intentional. He didn't want to think—worry—about what was in the cargo hold, not alone.

He rubbed his beard. It wasn't just that he was scared. The implications were simply too big, too important to start wondering what it meant—not until there were others to talk with.

Though he knew this . . . What was in the cargo hold of this airship was the most important discovery of modern times.

Bar none.

"Dr. Mlodinow?"

The German waiter tripped only slightly on his name, almost getting the opening blend of "me-lod."

Only took him three days . . .

"Yes?"

"*Mein Herr,* we are about to begin afternoon tea service. Would you care to order?"

He looked around. The parlor did double duty as a dining room, and the staff now scurried around preparing the tables for a tea service.

Stealing a page from the Brits, Mlodinow guessed.

Mile-high elegance, even as the fatherland marched into gothic madness.

"No, thank you. I think I'll lie down for a bit."

"Very good, *mein Herr.*"

Mlodinow stood up. He grabbed his cane and started walking out of the room to the central corridor of the zeppelin that led to the dozen staterooms. Every step brought a jolt of pain to his left leg, a pain so constant that Mlodinow had almost got to the point where he could ignore it.

Afternoon sun bathed the other side of the sitting room with golden light, making the wait staff glow brilliantly in their starched white outfits.

He pushed open the twin doors that led to the passengers' rooms.

The room was spacious, by ship standards.

Mlodinow knew that was because up here weight was the real problem.

He walked over to the slanted windows that looked down on the dark blue ocean below. He pulled closed a curtain, and the room slipped into a half-light.

He lay down on the bed. Maybe he'd nap—or maybe just lie there and think.

Tomorrow he'd land in Lakehurst and a small truck would meet him. The vehicle would take him and his cargo directly to the American Museum of Natural History on New York's Upper West Side.

The president's representative, a man named Robertson, would meet him there. And what did he hope would come out of this? What could happen?

From the moment when someone contacted him in Basel with the news of this find, his head had been spinning with the possibilities. He knew he wanted to get it out of Europe. Each day the climate there turned more mad, more dangerous.

This find could be a ticket to a life in the United States. Not a bad thing for a Jewish scientist. He had heard his grandfather talk about the bad old days, had the fear drilled into him.

And strange . . . he chose the *Graf Zeppelin.* Speed was important, but he wanted the specimen to get a special crate, special treatment. Being one of a handful of passengers guaranteed just that.

But finding a life in America wasn't the real reason that he made this journey. No. After the first tests on the specimen, he knew what he had to do.

People in power must know, they *must* understand the implications. And yes, the world seemed to be once again tottering toward chaos, maybe even racing to another world war—but still things had to be done.

A knock at the door.

"Ein bett, mein Herr?"

"Nein, bitte," Mlodinow said, not needing his covers turned down.

The German obsessiveness for everything to be done just so.

Mlodinow hoped that Hindenburg could keep that obsessiveness in check. The German moderates hoped that the old general would stop the country's wild spin to . . . to—

What?

That was just it. Who knew which small party, which sect would squeeze and fight and bully its way to power if Hindenburg didn't stop them?

But he was an old man. And the German people can be so persistent, so obsessive.

Better to stay in America, Mlodinow thought.

Let the world learn that things—that this planet—is not as they imagined. And let them learn that from America.

He squeezed his eyes shut—and tried to fall asleep as the propellers moved the airship smoothly through the clouds.

44

PRESTON PULLED CARL AWAY FROM Baxter.

"Hey, Preston, I'm talking to our star. Trying to keep him happy. Least I got him a costar. What's up?"

"Carl, there are two trucks outside with jungle trees and plants."

"Well, great, bring them in. Some of the sets are ready to be dressed. Maybe we can actually start doing some shooting."

"But there are supposed to be three trucks. *Three.* That's what I ordered."

"Oh, right. That's what you ordered, but I changed it."

"Can you tell me why? That's what the studio approved, that's what's in the budget—"

Denham fought hard to keep a smile off his face. "Exactly. That's what *they* approved. So, that's what they think we got."

"But you're only using two? And the money for the third truck?"

Now Denham walked Preston away from where anyone else might hear.

"Did you really think I was going to shoot a jungle movie with nothing but interiors and some phony-looking back-lot stuff? Did you really think that's what I was going to do? And that—" He looked right in Preston's eyes. Half the fun of moments like these was rattling his loyal but slow-to-catch-on assistant. "—that would still be a 'Carl Denham' movie?"

Preston licked his lips and pushed his glasses off his nose.

"You're pocketing the money?"

"Not pocketing. Every penny is going into the production, every penny, Preston. Just not exactly where the studio wants it to go—or thinks it's going. No matter, when they see the results, they'll be happy."

"And where is that money going?"

Denham looked left and right. "The *Venture* is going to wait. Englehorn is doing some repairs, holding off heading to Singapore or Sumatra for a zoo run. He's waiting . . ."

"Now I'm scared. He's waiting for what?"

"For me. I'm going to shoot some of these interiors. Got Jack Driscoll working on a new script for me too." He held his hands up. "Completely new. With some changes . . ."

"Like?"

"A voyage to someplace amazing, Preston. A beautiful girl, a dumb but equally beautiful actor. Danger, romance, and things people haven't seen before."

"And where exactly is that?"

"Can you keep a secret?"

"I'm your personal assistant, Carl. Who am I going to spill the beans to . . . you?"

"Okay. That place? I don't know. Yet."

"Great. And meanwhile we're paying for the *Venture*."

"At a good price. Englehorn, Hayes, Lumpy—they're all enjoying some time in New York."

"I would too if someone paid my freight. And how long—I mean, how much longer will you keep the ship waiting?"

"I've got to be a little careful, natch. If Zelman or one of his goons came to check things out, they got to see movie-making going on in this barn of a studio. I have to get some footage, some decent footage, to keep them happy. Meantime, I'm going to hunt for my destination."

"Really?"

"You know those bars in Brooklyn, near the Navy Yard?"

"No."

"Not your kind of places. But I went there, knowing that guys from the ships like to hang out, have a few bats and balls, talk to the floozies. Now, I got nothing yet, but some mug's gotta come in with some story about shipping out to some place amazing. And if I strike out there, then there are the dives over by the Hoboken piers. One way or another, I'll find a place."

"And I guess I shouldn't be surprised to see other items from the budget missing?"

"Could be, Preston, could be."

Herb shouted from across the open space of the studio. "We're set for you here, Carl."

Herb, limping a bit, but back to what he loved.

"Right. I'll be there in a second." He turned back to his assistant. "So, I just need to know, Preston—you're okay with this? You with me? 'Cause if you're not . . ."

Preston nodded. "Yes. I guess it wouldn't be a 'Carl Denham' picture of it didn't have that imminent sense of danger."

"Now you're thinking. And hey, I've got a scene to shoot. Take care of the foliage, will you?"

Preston nodded, as Denham hurried back to his cameraman.

45

Atlantic City, New Jersey

THE FIRST DAYS AFTER THE club attack turned into a blur for Ann . . . though Susan wouldn't stop talking about how Ann had saved her.

"I owe you, sister, big-time, and I ain't never gonna forget it," she kept saying. "Never!"

Ann wished she would. All she did, after all, was drag Susan out of there. Anyone could have done it. And while Susan talked about how "exciting" it all was, Ann more than ever felt that this was the wrong place for her.

But what else could she do? She certainly didn't have much of a nest egg to take back to New York and start auditioning . . . to try and get her acting life started again. The diving show would slowly give her a little savings . . . nothing to walk away from these days.

And guys?

Ann's experience with guys, anything approaching romance, wasn't ever good. Sooner or later you get disappointed, she thought. It's what her mother said, though Mom herself never stopped trying . . . guy after loser guy.

Maybe Ann had let herself become too hard, too well protected.

Or maybe she was one of the few who knew the score. Love was a chance to get hurt, an opportunity to get burned. She didn't want to get burned anymore.

So Ann kept diving, and planning for when her real life—as an actress—would truly begin.

Ann led Belle from the paddock, getting the dappled horse ready to dive. And she looked at his eyes.

Instead of the clear white pools surrounded by the bull's-eye brown pupils, the horse's eyes looked wet, and crisscrossed with red veins.

Belle didn't look good.

She went to Eddy and told him.

"Yeah," he said, taking a cigar out of his mouth. "I noticed. The horse has got a cold. Not surprising, with all the in and out of the water they got to do."

"Well, maybe she shouldn't dive."

"I gotta keep her in the rotation, kid—otherwise it's too much on the other horses. Besides, it's no big deal. Just a cold. We all get them."

"I don't know," Ann said. "She looks weak, tired."

Eddy looked up. "Okay. Tell you what. Let's see how she does with her first dive. If she looks bad, we'll talk about what we can do, okay Annie?"

Ann nodded. She started to turn away.

"And say, kid—how are you doing?"

Ann stopped, and turned back to the trainer. "Me? Fine. Okay."

He stood up. "Really? You can't tell me you aren't a bit rattled, after all that." He laughed. "I know I would be."

Ann forced a smile. "No. I was worried about my friends. But it happened so quickly, then we—" She laughed, genuine this time, remembering their flight from the club. "—we got the hell out of there."

Eddy grinned, nodding. "Bet you did, Annie, bet you did. But look, if you need someone to talk to, you know, just to *talk*—let me know. My eyes are kinda going—but I do have two good ears."

She reached out and gave his forearm a squeeze.

"Thanks. I'll remember that."

Then she turned and went back to Belle.

On the first dive, Belle seemed fine. She jumped smoothly, landed well in the ocean, slicing through the water, and quickly got out. Eddy thought that Belle could continue diving, even though Ann was still not sure—as though she could sense how the horse was doing inside.

Then on each subsequent dive, Ann felt a bit of hesitation from Belle, taking more time on the ramp, then a longer pause before jumping.

When Ann looked down at Eddy from the diving platform, she could see that now his face showed concern also.

After the last dive of the day, she went to him.

"She's not doing well."

"I see."

"So tomorrow off?"

"Maybe. Could be. I have to talk to Mr. Nadler. It will affect half the shows. You know people come here to see you and this horse. It's a big deal to disappoint them." He reached up and stroked the horse's neck. "I'll talk to Mr. Nadler. See what I can do. Get the vet to take a look."

"Thanks. Maybe a day off will get her back to normal."

And Ann thought, she too wouldn't mind a day off.

"Check in during the morning —and we'll see."

Ann showed up at the paddock early thinking that today she wouldn't be diving.

But she found Belle saddled up, and ready to go. Her eyes looked, if anything, worse. And she kept snorting as if now her nose was giving her problems.

"What did the vet say . . . and Mr. Nadler?"

"Look, kid, the Aquacade is an important part of the Steel Pier. And it's a weekend—gonna be jammed today."

"You mean Belle has to dive?"

"I'm afraid so."

"But what did the vet say?"

"Hell, he works for Nadler. So he's not going to give the boss bad news unless he has to. He said Belle has a cold, but it was nothing she wouldn't shake off . . . eventually."

" 'Shake off,' with all this diving? She'll only get worse."

"Sorry, Annie, I'm just an employee too. I gotta do what the boss says—and he says the horse dives, with or without you."

Ann looked at Belle. She'd gain nothing by refusing to dive with the horse. Some other girl could fill in. And she didn't want to be away from Belle, not when she looked so sick.

"I'll dive."

"Good. Better you're the one there, you know?"

"I know . . ."

The heat turned brutal, even at the end of the pier with the ocean surrounding the amphitheater. Now, when the wind blew off the ocean, the temperature made ribbony heat waves rise from every surface.

The audience had to be cooking in their seats below, trying to keep from touching any exposed metal.

As the announcer began her introduction, Ann climbed aboard Belle for the first dive of the day. Again the horse snorted, and Ann wondered whether the vet checked if Belle had equine flu. What would happen to her if she kept diving, not with a cold, but with an influenza that could kill her?

She leaned down to Belle.

"I'm with you, girl. Let's just take it nice and easy."

As if understanding her soothing words, Belle reared her head back, nuzzling Ann.

And to think that people thought Belle was difficult.

Sometimes, Ann guessed, there were things you could depend on: Belle on her, she . . . on Belle.

"Nice and easy, okay?"

The announcer finished, they started up the ramp. Ann could feel that each step was labored, that the horse had a hard time even lifting one leg up and moving it forward.

This is wrong, she thought.

After this, she'd stop it—one way or the other.

Now the brilliant morning sun hit them both, and the heat felt as though someone had opened the door to an oven.

More snorts—the heat had to be making the horse feel worse.

Still Belle climbed up to the platform, as Ann kept stroking its neck, whispering, "Thatta girl . . . almost there . . . almost done. . . ."

The horse reached the platform, and turned.

Ann remembered to turn to the audience and wave while the announcer directed all eyes to the amazing feat that was about to occur.

"Okay. Let's do this dive. One dive . . ."

Ann almost didn't have the heart to give it the kick to its flanks to set her leap into motion. But it was the cue—Belle needed it.

But Ann knew she'd make it as gentle as possible, while still being clear it was time.

She leaned down to the horse and again whispered, "Ready, girl?"

Another tilt of the head back and—

Ann kicked her heels into the horse's flanks.

Belle stepped back for the jump. Ann heard something.

The horse started urinating, a stream of water coating the platform, something that never happened before, more evidence of just how sick the horse was.

Ann considered grabbing the reins to stop the horse, but it all happened too quickly, like a machine set in motion, irreversible.

Belle started racing to the edge of the platform, struggling for the speed that would send it flying safely out into space, and into the ocean.

Hooves thumping, speeding over the now wet platform toward the edge.

When Belle suddenly slipped.

The horse tilted left, then went crashing down. But it was too late to stop the jump, and Belle kept careering forward. Ann quickly looked down and back, to see Belle's left leg twisted under her body. She saw some red, a bit of bony white.

And then the two of them went sliding off the platform, Belle actually spinning so that Ann felt the horse *above* her as they plummeted to the water. Still she held on, as they crashed into the ocean.

The deadweight of the horse smashed down, pushing Ann deeper under the water than she'd ever been.

She let go of the bridle, pushing away, kicking away, realizing that all the air had been kicked out of her.

She broke the surface.

For a second she didn't see Belle. Then the horse's head, nostrils flaring, eyes wild with terror, also broke the surface. Belle started paddling to where she could get out of the sea.

But she paddled so slowly.

Ann hurried to Eddy, waiting. She pushed herself out of the water, and stood up, watching the struggling animal fight her way to the platform.

The announcer started telling the audience that everything was okay. That they shouldn't worry. Then, just as Belle reached the platform, eyes nearly bugging out of her head, the announcer told the audience that the show was over, to please leave quietly.

So they wouldn't see, Ann thought . . . so they wouldn't *see* what Belle looked like when they finally got her out of the water.

It had taken Eddy and two other men to help Belle out, and Ann immediately saw the right rear leg, twisted at an odd angle, a chunk of bone sticking out. Belle made a terrible moaning sound—once, twice—and then laid her head down on the board-walk floor, and breathed deeply as if she couldn't get enough air.

Ann crouched close by, stroking her head.

By now Nadler and the vet were there.

The vet stood at a distance, as though he didn't want to be connected to what was his handiwork. Ann turned to them both.

"You did this. You made her dive."

Nadler started to say something . . . "Ann, I—"

"You killed her."

She fought back tears. She wanted them to feel her anger, her disgust—and not just her girlish tears.

And when she couldn't fight anymore, she leaned into the horse's heaving head so no one would see the tears as they started to flow.

Ann heard a click.

The vet stood there with a rifle.

She turned around.

"No. You can't—"

Even though Ann knew there was no other way. Eddy crouched down.

"Ann, you know it has to be done. . . ."

Her head still against the animal's head, she nodded. *Nothing lasts,* she thought for the hundredth time. *Everything can be taken away from you.*

Eddy tightened his grip on her shoulder, then pulled her away. Slowly she released her hold on the horse's neck, and allowed herself to be pulled to a standing position.

The vet moved closer, and aimed the gun at Belle's head.

"Maybe you . . . want to go away? We can wait," the vet said.

But Ann, eyes burning, shook her head.

Nadler nodded to the vet.

He raised the rifle.

A moment's hesitation, with the barrel close, aimed right at Belle's head.

The click, the explosion—and then it was over.

46

On an uncharted island
NO ONE IN THE CAVE MOVED.

Sam looked at the girl cowering, her eyes wide. She didn't match any image of a native Sam had seen. Her hair was straight, a lustrous brown but matted with mud. The color of her skin was nearly bronze.

Who is she . . . what is she?

And it was clear that she didn't trust him. If she pressed any closer to the wall of the cave, she'd melt into it. . . .

The dinosaur, the mammoth *V. rex,* still patrolled outside, marching back and forth. Every now and then they'd see its giant foot, claws grasping outward, land right in front of the opening.

Sam thought of one good thing about having it outside: nothing smaller could sneak into the opening, something smaller . . . nastier.

Because Sam was sure that on this hell island, such things had to exist.

And what else?

The other men also lay still, and Sam imagined

that they were quiet out of a combination of fear and shock.

He looked out the opening. The light outside was fading. Night was close.

Do we really want to be here when it turns dark?

As if in answer to his thoughts, a giant foot landed outside the opening. He heard a bit of a snort.

I wonder how patient a dinosaur can be?

"Turn on your lights," Sam said.

He said it quietly, but it was an order. He was in charge now. Getting them out of this would be his job.

Rosa clipped on his flashlight, and it made a pale yellow light.

"Shit, batteries," Sam said.

He imagined that the other flashlight from Bakali would be in the same half-dead state.

Bakali turned it on, and a bright light shot out of the foot-long flashlight.

"This one . . . is good," he said.

Then Jorge turned on the last flashlight, and it too sent out a bright light. Jorge waved it around, a quick glance into the gloom of the cave.

Sam looked at the ground.

"Somebody's been here. Look."

On the ground, the imprint of shoes, a waffle shape—certainly not something from the natives.

Did that crew end up here, or some other trapped sailors?

Another thought that made Sam's stomach go tight.

Could it be something on this island, something here that killed them?

Then he looked up at the cave walls . . . to see:

Images.

"Hold on!" Sam said. "Let me see."

He extended his hand to take the flashlight, but Jorge pulled it close, reluctant to let the precious light source go.

"Give it to him," Rosa barked.

Jorge slowly, reluctantly handed the light to Sam.

He turned and pointed it at the wall opposite them, an area that had just been briefly illuminated.

Now, the light cast a yellow blotch on the wall, and Sam moved the blotch, tracing through the painted images.

Some of the strange images meant nothing. He saw what looked like more eerie statues, carved images. Someone replicating idols maybe, drawing them in the cave?

Maybe praying to those faces while they too were stalked by something outside.

Then other images, dinosaurs, attacking, eating— something remembered? And other creatures, winged things with ratlike heads, but drawn as big as some of the dinosaurs.

Things that never existed. *Or maybe—we just* thought *that they never existed.*

"What is this?" Rosa said.

Sam turned, keeping the light down so as not to blind anyone.

"I don't know. Cave drawings. Someone else has been here. They're old. Maybe . . . ancient."

He turned back to the wall, letting his light trail farther into the darkness.

"Hold on. What's this?" he said. He went closer. For a moment it looked like the drawing of a crab, or a lobster, then—when Sam turned his head—one end looked like a skull.

He put his fingers on it.

He saw a bit he recognized, a stretch of the outlined shape that was familiar.

It was the *island*.

"It's the island. This is a map of the island." The others came and stood by him. "See, here's where we landed."

Rosa translated for the crew who spoke no English.

"We landed here, so we are here. And the jungle reaches there, to—"

He followed what appeared to be a ridge that ran close to the shore. An oddly shaped mountain that hugged the shore, leading to a small mountain range. . . .

Looking closer, Sam saw that whoever drew this image showed plumes of smoke gushing out of the mountaintop.

A volcano.

Great, we're near an active volcano.

Just when things couldn't get any better.

Sam turned to Rosa.

"You carrying any paper?"

"I always keep copies of my charts with me."

"Let me have one."

Rosa hesitated.

"Come on," Sam barked.

Rosa reluctantly dug into a large side pocket and pulled out a folded wad of paper. He peeled off one of the folded charts and handed it to Sam.

The floor was littered with charred bits of wood, wood turned jet black, into charcoal. He ripped his shirt until he had a nearly square piece.

He gave Jorge back his flashlight.

"Hold this. Keep it on the map."

And looking up, Sam grabbed some of the blackened wood and then began copying the map of the island, their prison, onto the back of the thick, parchmentlike paper.

"What are you doing that for?" Rosa asked.

"I imagine if we are to get off this damn island, having a map might be useful."

He didn't say his other reason for copying the map.

If they got off . . . *If they got away . . .*

His eyes followed the strange outline of the island.

He felt movement behind him. The girl. She crept close, slowly. Sam looked back at her. She seemed curious about what he was doing, now not afraid any longer.

She came up beside Sam and looked down just as his drawing was done. He put some swirls around the island to indicate the fog.

Done.

She shook her head, A universal language, *yes, no . . . wrong*.

She reached out, tiny fingers, all scratched from whatever ordeal she had been through.

She took the charcoal and then pointed to a spot on the island. Then she spoke: *"Nore la . . . tore. Kong ka! Tore . . . lama Kong!"* She turned and looked at Sam. Her thin lips mouthed a word again. . . .

"Kong . . ."

And she drew on a corner of the map. She drew a face. At first Sam thought that it was just another idol face, that the girl was simply doing something to acknowledge the gods who put her into such a god-awful situation.

But then, when she was done, he could see that the face was that of an ape, a gorilla.

She said the word again . . . *"Kong . . ."*

Sam repeated the odd word, a word that almost seemed to have a strange power.

"Kong?"

Jorge shut off the light, and then rattled off some Portuguese.

Three of the crew gathered together, talking, planning.

Sam stood up and went to Rosa, giving the girl a look and a nod. "What are they saying?"

"They think there may be another way out of here."

"Out of here. How the hell—"

Rosa gestured to the interior of the cave. "Through there, maybe another way out, another way out and back to the ship."

"Or maybe they'll get lost."

Rosa spit on the ground. "Better than staying here."

Sam started to say something. But what? How good were their chances with the giant carnivore on guard outside?

"Yeah. Okay. Who?"

"Jorge, Luis . . . they take one flashlight. If they find something, they come back and tell us." Rosa turned and spoke to Jorge.

"Tell them fifteen minutes. Then they should be back."

Wouldn't it be great if they split up? Nice way to have this whole thing turn even deadlier.

As he stood there, the girl came beside him, secretly, in the shadows; he felt her tiny hand grab his.

That's one ally I got, he thought.

"Okay," Rosa said. "They're ready."

A rumble echoed from outside. Not the roar of the dinosaur, but thunder, a storm beginning as the light faded from this island of the skull.

Sam made three flashes of five with his hand. "Fifteen minutes?" he said to them.

Then Jorge and Luis set off.

Jorge felt Luis walking right next to him while he made the flashlight sway back and forth.

"Frigida, sí?"

"Si . . ." said Jorge.

The cave turned cold, and now Jorge's sweat made him feel chilled, icy.

And as the cave tunnel chilled, it narrowed, so now they had to crouch down, stooped over, marching through the tunnel.

It certainly didn't seem like a way out. But then—suddenly—the narrow chute opened up.

Jorge turned to Luis and grinned.

"Bueno . . ."

The tunnel opened up into a large irregular cavern. Jorge quickly scanned the cavern, and his light picked up a chunk of rock that glistened and glowed even with the flashlight off it. But under the light, the rock glowed with a color that Jorge had never seen.

It filled the cavern.

And Jorge thought: *Maybe this is valuable. Maybe this will make us wealthy. When we get off the island.*

Because certainly they would get off the island.

With Luis still glued, he walked over to a boulder-sized chunk of the odd outcrop.

There were some loose pieces that he picked up, glowing in his hand. Then both he and Luis touched the boulder.

"Stupendo, Luis, no?"

He looked up. With an opening this large, surely it must lead to a way out.

He let his light swing around the cavern, when it picked up something moving.

Moving, then vanished. He searched again, the light circling around, like a moth drawn to a summer light.

Then again, more fast movement . . .

Only now the thing that moved stopped atop one boulder so they could see it.

And Jorge felt Luis's hand dig into his forearm.

47

On an uncharted island

JORGE SHRUGGED OFF LUIS'S VISELIKE GRIP.

The insectile thing on the rock was as long as a man. The head had twin pincers, and a row of legs ran down a body as thick as a tree trunk.

It looked right at them, the pincers opening and closing in slow motion. With the light on it, Jorge could see that the legs ended in hooks that looked as dangerous as the head pincers.

Like an insect he'd find scurrying on the floor of a fishing hut, no bigger than a thumbnail.

"Luis," Jorge whispered. *"Vámonos . . ."*

He started to turn around. The thing could move fast, but it was still far away. They could get back to the narrow tunnel, back to the others, still be safe.

He turned around.

And between them and the opening, he could see twenty, thirty, maybe *more* of these things, all sizes, but not one shorter than the length of his arm—all with their pincers waving.

He heard water.

Luis was urinating as he stood there.

Jorge began to pray, to the Son of God, to His Mother, the Virgin.

Because when those things moved, there was not even time for a prayer.

The storm raged outside, sending down a wall of water.

Outside the cave puddles bloomed, then the puddles turned into ponds. When Sam edged closer, to look outside as lightning flashed, he could still see the dinosaur.

They were still trapped.

The girl stayed close to him. No one said anything about it, no one questioned her holding on to Sam.

The map was tucked deep into his pants pocket.

"It's been more than fifteen minutes . . ." Sam said to Rosa.

"Yes. You are right. What . . . do we do?"

Good question that. He turned to Bakali. "Give me your light."

Bakali shook his head. "My light. Get your own."

He took a step closer to Bakali.

"Your light. *Por favor.*"

Bakali handed Sam the light. Then Sam unhooked the girl from his hand, which she quickly reattached. He shook his head, *no.* He said the word. "No."

But she shook her head back.

"Okay," he nodded.

He turned back to the others, "I'm going to go in a bit . . . to see if they are on the way—"

A giant clap of thunder, and all of their eyes in the half-light went wide. It was turning into a storm beyond anything any one of them had ever heard.

"Okay. I'm going in. . . ."

Sam started down the tunnel with the girl in tow.

The light was still bright, but Sam knew they didn't have much time. They would have to do something soon.

He heard a sound and stopped.

The first insect thing appeared, corkscrewing its way toward them, then another.

The light made them stop. From the massive sound of chittering, there had to be dozens more coming.

The light showed one of the pincers with a red smear.

That . . . answers that, Sam thought.

Jorge, Luis.

He grabbed the girl's hand and turned back, running hard.

The thunderous storm meant that Sam had to scream to be heard.

"We have to leave!"

But Rosa didn't understand, so Sam yelled again. "We have to leave *now*!"

"But what about Jorge? What about—"

One of the crewmen yelled.

Sam spun around with the light.

The first of the things, the giant insects, was there—and had curled around one of the crewmen.

They watched what happened—blazingly fast.

The pincers grabbed the small crewman's body, and the flesh began flying off, as if the man was being peeled layer by layer. The insect chewed as it cut, but others had appeared, pausing now to grab chunks of the flayed skin and muscle.

Sam handed Bakali his light, which wouldn't make a difference anymore.

He looked at the girl. She squeezed his hand painfully tight. But Sam didn't doubt that she knew what had to happen.

"Now!" he yelled out to the wall of water, the flashing lightning, the rolling waves of thunder.

As soon as the four of them emerged, the roar of thunder was joined by a new sound—the dinosaur's bellow.

Fortunately it had been prowling at the far end, closer to the jungle.

They had a dozen meters' lead on it.

Not much. But maybe—Christ!—maybe it would be enough.

Sam ran full out, the rain so heavy that it was hard to breathe. The puddles had turned into slippery ponds.

He heard the dinosaur roar, now aimed right at them.

Then—not from the sky, not from the dinosaur—another great roar.

Deep, rumbling, challenging all the other sounds.

The girl yelled out the word again.

"Kong!"

Whatever made that sound . . .

That—was Kong.

Bakali was just behind them, Rosa a few steps behind.

Not breaking his stride, Sam looked back as they reached the paths that girded the cliff. The creature wasn't as fast as he feared, trudging more slowly through the mud pools.

But then he saw Rosa slip in one of the new pools.

The *V. rex* had moved more slowly than Sam thought it would; but now it also moved in a way that seemed impossible. Almost like a snake, it lowered its massive head nearly to the ground, tilting forward, its legs somehow letting its upper torso become almost horizontal.

It scooped up Rosa like a steam shovel grabbing a ton of rock.

Rosa's screaming head was the last thing to vanish into the gigantic maw.

The act gave Sam, Bakali, and the young girl more time.

"Come on!" he yelled, the girl holding on to him, Bakali bug-eyed.

They ran through a dense stand of trees. It was possible that the dinosaur would be stopped by the foliage . . . but Sam didn't want to take any chances.

He kept running to the ledge.

For now, any thoughts of repairing the ship vanished.

The heavy rain had created a dozen small streams that cascaded down the ledge, tumbling over the rocks. Sam scanned the ledge looking for a way down.

One section, filled with a jumble of sharp-edged, table-sized boulders, looked navigable.

He pulled the girl in that direction, and a few steps behind, Bakali followed.

48

On an uncharted island

THEY HALF-CLIMBED, HALF-SLIPPED DOWN the rocky
slope made glassy by the downpour.

Every few seconds, another lightning bolt would
flash, and Sam could see the next few feet clearly,
avoiding the sharp edges that had already cut jagged
red lines into his hand.

He saw Bakali slip, falling backward, then yelling as
his head smacked backward, hard onto one of the rocks.

He looked to see if he needed help, but Bakali scurried up quickly.

Near the bottom, the girl slipped too and her hand
slid away. But—so fast—she hurried to grab Sam's
hand again.

The climb down seemed to take forever. Until, so
unexpected, they were at the bottom.

The crewman who was supposed to be by the
dinghy was gone.

Water streaming off his face, Sam looked around.
Where the hell could the crewman be? Bakali looked
too, searching as the lightning lit up the shore.

Then the answer came.

*   *   *

The flying reptile swooped out of nowhere.

It had a long, U-shaped head, and a sleek body with two clawlike legs.

This one looks like a goddamn vulture! Sam thought.

First it locked its jaw around Bakali's neck. That didn't kill him, as Bakali tried to scream. But his air supply was cut off and Bakali just kept opening his mouth like a fish, trying to speak, trying to make any sound.

The creature's wings flapped, but Bakali must have been too heavy for it.

Sam pulled out his gun.

But much too slowly, for the reptile now dug its two claw feet into Bakali's midsection, and opened him up.

In a second, the trapped man's body lay completely open.

As the "Vulturesaurus" released Bakali's head, Sam fired two shots at where he imagined its brain must be. The creature howled in agony. It tried to flap its wings and escape, but after three short flaps, it fell forward, dead.

"We gotta go," Sam said. He started pulling the girl to the boat. Had she ever seen a boat, did she know what this was?

She stepped into the dinghy, and Sam pushed it off the shore. He hurried to the center bench seat and started rowing as fast as he could. The storm had turned the water into something choppy, boiling. The boat rocked up and down, dipping below the water—

and for every three great pulls on the oars, Sam imagined that he lost as much as half the ground.

He also kept checking the skies above.

But so far, no more flying dinosaurs.

It's absurd, he thought. *Flying dinosaurs.*

Life changes so quickly, reality shifts bizarrely in an instant.

He bumped against the *Susana.*

He quickly tied the rowboat to the stern, and jumped aboard.

He saw the girl, bobbing in the boat, looking at it as if it was as frightening as the creature he just killed.

"Come on," he said. "It's okay."

She looked right at Sam and then, in what must have been an act of trust, she climbed aboard.

He didn't have time to pull the anchors up; he took his knife and cut each, then dragged the girl into the wheelhouse. He could hear the pumps below, still working to keep the churning ocean out of the ship.

Now he started the main engines, as the ship bobbed perilously close to the rocky shore.

He pressed the starter, but nothing happened.

"Damn . . ."

He hit it again, and then again, and then finally the engines kicked in. He cut the wheel hard to starboard, and pulled back on the throttle.

The ship started moving away from the rocks.

Even though he knew he was moving away from the shore, he could see almost nothing.

His hands gripped the wheel hard.

The ship moved sluggishly—obviously the sea had gained on the pumps, or maybe all the rocking had made the gash worse.

Come on, come on, come on, Sam thought. *Just get us away from this hellhole.*

He looked back at the girl, standing beside him, by the door to the wheelhouse.

Sam gave the terrified girl a smile, then turned back to the windshield, a blackish blur.

They were safe from the rocks, the boat was moving away from the shore, even though it sat so low. Belowdecks probably awash with the sea.

How long before the water killed the engines? But they were off the island. About as close to being safe as he could ever hope.

Then—the ship hit something hard, and tilted sharply to starboard.

Sam had to hold on to the wheel as the ship kicked over at a sharp angle.

But the girl had been standing by the wheelhouse door, and it flew open with a jolt.

Sam turned—to see her go flying out, sprawling to the floor.

The ship quickly righted. She was in no danger of getting thrown overboard. Sam let go of the wheel.

To help her.

To bring her back.

And he thought, *It must have been waiting, hovering, circling the ship in the storm.*

The Vulturesaurus landed on the girl. Her eyes glistened in the flashing lightning. Not showing fear. Whatever had happened to her, she had passed fear a long time ago. Not really expecting that she would ever get away.

The creature's claw feet held her pinned. She reached out a hand to Sam. Since they had met, she had barely let him go.

The Vulturesaurus started flapping, and with the lighter girl, it started to rise in the air.

Sam had three bullets left in the gun. He held it out and emptied all three of the chambers at the thing.

Until its leathery wings stopped moving, and it fell a foot or so back to the deck.

He knelt down to the girl. She opened her mouth, and said words in her language. *"Ka-neh, ry-leh nah."* Then, softly, so that Sam had to put his ear next to her lips, *"Ka-neh . . ."*

Then the light went out of her eyes.

Sam saw one of the creature's claw feet still buried in the girl's body. He reached down and began pulling it out. One claw caught on something, a bit of bone.

Maybe, Sam thought, *it was damaged before, in some other attack.*

The loose claw popped free and fell to the deck.

Sam picked it up and put it back in his pocket.

The ship moved sluggishly in the churning sea. Sam

went back to the wheelhouse, wondering, *And how much longer do I have?*

The *Susana* passed into the fog bank, and then started out of the other side when the engines stopped.

Sam still held on to the wheel. Water crashed onto the deck, great choppy waves sloshing over the wood from either side.

The ship sat low in the water; it was sinking.

He let go of the wheel. He took a few deep breaths, trying to think.

He took out the map that he had made—miraculously, it hadn't gotten too wet. On the other side, it showed their course west of Sumatra. He flipped it back over and grabbed a black oil marker. He wrote down the longitude and latitude. He carefully folded the map up and put it back in his pocket. He was alone. Everyone else was gone. He was alone, but he was alive.

Sam walked out of the wheelhouse, and ran to the stern. The ship rocked left and right, taking huge gulps of sea water, but also at the same time spinning, as if in a vortex.

He reached the dinghy, also with about a half-foot of water but riding the crazy surf better than the dive ship.

He jumped into the rowboat and untied it. A trough sent him slamming to the seat. He grabbed the oars. Then free of the sinking ship, he began fighting the sea with the oars, cursing, screaming, bellowing back at the thunder.

Until—

At some point he noticed that the thunder was gone, the lightning was gone, the rain had stopped.

The sun was out, and only he was making any noise, still yelling at the top of his lungs.

The sun seemed to hang overhead as though it was immovable. A brilliant white-hot lamp aimed down only on him.

He stopped rowing when he realized he had no idea where he was headed. Besides, it seemed easier to sit in the boat and let the sun do its work.

49

Atlantic City, New Jersey

WHEN ANN CAME BACK TO the apartment, it was afternoon; the late summer sun cut through the back windows sending a golden light that cut through all the rooms.

No one was there, and she was just as glad.

She could pack, get all set before the good-byes and leaving. It hadn't been hard telling Nadler that she was moving on.

Though she hadn't saved a lot of money, she did have some. Enough, maybe, to go back to New York and start knocking on doors again.

Something would turn up. Something had to.

She walked into the kitchen to get a drink of water. The envelope was on the table, and a piece of paper next to it.

"Ann, this came for you . . . Ellie," was scrawled on the paper.

The envelope bore the words WESTERN UNION, and the familiar yellow color of a telegram.

She checked in the glassine window to see that the blocky letters did indeed spell her name.

ANN DARROW.

She opened it, and pulled out the oddly folded message, reading:

ANN
GET YOUR BAGGYPANTS OUT NOW STOP
NEW SHOW NEEDS US STOP
COME BACK TO MANHATTAN STOP
LOVE MANNY STOP

Ann read it again just to make sure that the words wouldn't vanish, that the words were in fact real.

And then, finally, she sat down on one of the kitchen chairs and, in the golden light, with no one there, no one to see, she openly wept.

50

The Indian Ocean

HENNING MENKEL YAWNED.

This stretch of the sea could be so boring; a big empty ocean. His freighter runs had become so routine that he almost felt the ship had no need of a captain.

Perhaps he could turn the ship over to his first mate and catch a nap.

That sounded good, a nice long sleep while the ship steamed over the still sea.

He rubbed his eyes. Tired, maybe a little old for this, he thought. Might be time to head back to Norway and give up the sea.

Was that even possible? he thought. *Was there any kind of life there for me?*

He blinked.

He saw a dot on the ocean.

Must be a bit of wood, something kicked up by a storm?

He reached down for his binoculars.

It was a boat. A boat bobbing on the endless flat sea.

"Cut hard to port, Eric," he said to the man at the wheel. "And slow a third."

Another look through the binoculars.

No doubt—a rowboat. Was there someone in it? Where the hell did a rowboat come from out here? There had been no radio reports of ships in trouble.

Now the freighter steamed to the bobbing boat, and Captain Menkel started giving orders for the boat to be recovered . . . and to see what might be in it.

Menkel stood at the rail as his men tied up the boat and brought someone out of the boat, then up the walkway to the main deck.

Two crewmen held up the man, his skin festering with blisters, lips parched to a bloated, papery whiteness.

But the man opened his eyes. Still alive. Cooked like a piece of bacon, but still alive.

"Hello?" Menkel said to the man in heavily accented English.

One of the crew took a wet towel and dabbed at the man's lips. They'd have to give him water slowly.

The man opened his lips, trying to speak.

At first Menkel could hear nothing, just small puffs of air that somehow escaped the parched mouth.

But then, indeed . . . words. . . .

Epilogue

JACK DRISCOLL POURED ANOTHER FEW fingers of bourbon. He read over what he had written, and then crumpled the page into a ball and threw it to the floor.

He looked over at the pages on his bureau.

Maybe I should get back to that, he thought . . . back to the story he promised Carl. Because one thing was for sure: Carl Denham wouldn't let him rest until he got *something.*

Except—what was in front of Jack was his real work.

But there was a problem. The characters in this new play seemed to be in their own separate worlds. Sure they talked to each other, supposedly cared about each other. *But I'm not buying it,* Driscoll thought. *And if I don't buy it, how can an audience?*

Another sip. The booze didn't help the writing—he wasn't that deluded. But maybe he could figure out what was missing from these people, what was wrong—

No. Not with them.

With me. Something missing in me.

How can you give characters something you don't have yourself?

Carl had nailed it when he told him, "Jack, you have to live if you want to write."

Live . . .

How does one do that?

Jack got up.

Got to be an answer somewhere.

He left his small apartment, without an idea of where he was going or what he'd do.

When Denham's production shut down for a few weeks, the director had his opportunity.

A plan.

If there was some place out there, an unknown island in the unknown seas, there might just be one place to find it.

Singapore!

The harbor bars back in the New York area had all come up dry, so he confided in no one when he left—after all, he might well come home empty-handed.

After a few days in the crowded port, haunting the watering holes that ringed the harbor, it looked as if this trip, this search for an island that didn't exist on the maps—an island that might be that most rare of things . . . *unknown*—just didn't exist at all.

Then he got a tip from a sailor, someone who had traveled with Denham years ago. A tip, a rumor . . . all for the price of some shots of cheap gin.

There was somebody there who might actually have what Denham was looking for. A Norwegian ship captain who had been talking in the bars.

It also wouldn't be the first time Denham had chased a bit of information only to have it vanish before his eyes. Tonight—his last night before returning home—would probably be the same.

The bar was called the Blue Rose. The *s* on the neon sign was out, and the darkness within made this the least appealing of the row of dingy bars that lined the street, drawing in the hard-drinking sailors, and the floozies at the ready to help relieve them of any money they might have left.

Dark inside, like a cave.

He took a breath. The man sat in the back, barely visible in the shadows. Carl walked over to the bartender. A plump blonde sat sprawled on a stool, her predatory eyes locked on him.

"Just a beer, please," he said. The bartender pulled back on the spigot and filled a glass with warm beer. Carl put down a few coins, then walked to the back of the bar.

"Mind if I sit down?"

"No."

The Norwegian captain had been told that Carl would be coming.

"Carl Denham," Carl said, extending his hand.

The captain shook it. "Henning Menkel."

"You're the captain of a freighter?"

A nod.

"And you found something? Something that I might be interested in?"

"Could be, Denham. Could be."

In the half-light, Denham could see that the captain's eyes were bloodshot. He'd obviously had a few before Carl's arrival. For a moment, neither said anything.

The guy seemed awfully secretive about his find. Carl didn't let his hopes get up. . . .

"Want to tell me about it?"

The man rubbed his beard.

"Weeks ago. We found a boat, just floating. It was nowhere. Not near an island, no ship's reported missing. At least not yet."

"Someone in it?"

Another nod. "A man half-dead. His skin cooked by the sun, delirious. Half-dead . . ."

"But not dead?"

"No. He lived for a few more hours. We gave him medicine for the pain. Some water. But no way could he live. But he spoke."

The captain's eyes started to water.

Christ, he's back there, Denham thought. *He's back in the open sea of the Indian Ocean as he tells me this.*

"It was crazy, mad talk. Said everyone else was killed. He said they were eaten, ripped apart by monsters. Crazy talk. I told him to stop. Got him some more water, got his burnt body some ointment. There wasn't much we could do. It's only a freighter, our infirmary just doesn't—"

"I understand."

The captain reached out and grabbed Carl's arm.

"But later, when I was alone with him, he started again. Babbling . . . an island that no one knew about. A island shaped like . . . a skull. The Island of the Skull, he said."

As the captain spoke, Carl's heart began racing.

If this was true, if it was real, then he might be on to something that could make this movie, make his secret plan turn into the most incredible Denham picture ever.

If it was true . . .

"But you said he sounded delirious, that he sounded crazy?"

The captain nodded. "I would have just . . . how do you say it . . . let it go. The sun can drive a man mad. But—"

The captain opened up a cracked leather satchel that he had beside him and brought out a folded piece of parchment paper.

"He had this."

The captain didn't unfold it.

"A map. Showing the island. With longitude, latitude. Skull Island."

"But it still could be . . . a delusion."

And in the shadows, Carl saw the captain smile, his brownish yellow teeth capturing a bit of the scant light.

"Yes. I thought that too. But then, deep inside his pocket, he also had this—"

The captain reached into his satchel again, grabbed something, and then let it fall to the table.

It was a claw.

Denham had made films using animals from around the world.

In size, in shape, in its deadly curl that ended in a needle-sharp hook, he had never seen a claw like that.

"God. What is it?"

The captain nodded. "Exactly, Mr. Denham. What is it?"

Denham picked up the claw.

He closed his fist on it, then opened it again.

Still there.

It was real.

"He said one word when I took this from him. One." The captain killed his whiskey.

"Kong. . . ."

Carl walked out of the Blue Rose, out to the rainy, steamy streets of the Singapore harbor. He felt giddy. This was incredible.

He had to pay more for the map than he planned, a lot more. But despite his pleas, the captain wouldn't part with the claw.

"Not for sale," the captain had said.

Perhaps the captain wanted to keep it so that he'd have some evidence that it was real too, that he wasn't mad. No matter.

And when the captain finally unfolded the map, when he brought the candle on the table close to the map, Denham saw the strange-shaped island.

The ridge that ran down one side close to the

shore. A mountainous outcrop—probably a volcanic rise. Might even be an active volcano there. The island also had twin hooklike spits of land that extended out of the island into the sea, as if grabbing for it.

It was unlike anything he had ever seen.

But he noticed the smudge on one corner. At first it didn't look like more than some stray black marks, circular. But when he turned the material around, he saw a face, of an ape or a gorilla of some kind.

"What's that?"

"I don't know. I don't know if the man knew."

Denham touched the image then.

And he said the word himself: "Kong . . ."

Now, walking beside the dock, the waters flowing out to the Asia, Europe, Africa, and beyond.

Denham had the map, the location. But there was much he had to do before he could leave. Preparations, because—even if the man had been crazy—Denham had seen the claw.

So there would be weapons.

Anything and everything he needed.

Destiny, he thought, had just delivered him the key to what would be the adventure of his life.

It would be hours before he could go to sleep, and with the next day he'd leave and the planning could really begin.

Robertson walked around the specimen.

They stood in the basement of the American Museum of Natural History, in a room used to assemble the museum's largest specimens of creatures long gone.

Mlodinow had been met by a truck, which took him from the *Graf Zeppelin* and the Lakehurst docking station directly to the museum.

While they met, Robertson asked the museum director if he could meet with Mlodinow by himself.

"How long would you say it is?"

Mlodinow looked down at the bones of the sea creature spread out on the massive table. "Forty . . . maybe fifty feet. The head alone is five—"

"Yes, I see. Gigantic." Robertson reached out and let his hand trail along the row of razor-sharp teeth. "Frightening."

"Yes. Which is why—"

Robertson looked up, and interrupted. "Who else knows about this?"

"I've only communicated with the White House, you, sir, and of course the museum."

Robertson nodded. "I've already spoken to the director. So that's not a worry—"

"I don't understand. Worry?"

"We—and I speak for the president—don't think that this information is something that would be good for the public to hear. At least right now."

Mlodinow's eyes went wide. "But, sir—this creature. The fact that it exists, that—"

Robertson picked up a stack of papers near the head of the creature.

"Right. I see all your tests here. You're sure that there's no mistake?"

"No."

"That it is a plesiosaur, a creature extinct for sixty million years, that its bones are less than . . . five years old. That it died less than five years ago?"

"Yes, it's all there. I tested many times. The creature was alive five years ago. And that's why——"

Robertson walked up to Mlodinow.

"Why . . . what?"

"If this was alive, if there's a place where prehistoric creatures somehow survived, then we need to find that place, protect that place——"

Robertson shook his head. "Do you understand what's going on in this country? The people out of work, the Depression? There's no money to go hunting for this place, even if it did exist, even if this thing wasn't alone."

"It couldn't be alone; the whole niche from the Jurassic period had to——"

"I know. It couldn't live in isolation. Listen, Dr. Mlodinow . . . I will speak to the museum director. I will arrange for you to stay in the United States. But nothing can be done now, and for now——nothing should be said . . . about this."

Again his hands touched the skull of the sea creature.

"Until?"

"Who knows. But for now, your prehistoric skeleton

just won't get the attention of the U.S. government. I doubt I could get anyone very excited about a bunch of bones; take more than that." Robertson took a breath. "Do you understand?"

Mlodinow nodded.

Nothing could be done for now.

"Good. I must go back now. But I will be in touch."

He shook hands with Mlodinow, then turned and left the cavernous room.

Leaving Mlodinow with his specimen. Thinking, *Could it be one of a kind, a fluke, some anomaly of nature?*

Or is there someplace out there where time had stopped sixty million years ago?

Would he ever get an answer to that question?

Somehow, standing alone in the basement room with this prehistoric monster from the sea, somehow he thought . . .

Oh, yes . . . that question will be answered.

And when he finally walked out of the castlelike museum building, it was a crisp dawn, with a deep cloudless sky and the sun just beginning to warm the sleepy streets of New York City.

About the Author

MATTHEW COSTELLO's innovative work includes groundbreaking and award-winning novels, games, and television shows. His latest novel, *Missing Monday,* was published in 2004 and was recently optioned for television. His novel *Beneath Still Waters* has been filmed for Lions Gate and Filmax for worldwide release in 2006. Costello has also scripted dozens of bestselling games, including the critically acclaimed The 7th Guest and Doom 3, of which *Time* magazine said, "To play Doom 3 is to feel your skin prickle with atavistic fear. The story is delivered with unusual art." He lives in New York.